Michael'
body as
him, her elbows on the counter, her hands
holding her glass.

His upper body leaned in so Stephanie was close enough for him to feel her heat. His hand was now on her upper arm, tugging her gently closer so her body was lined up against his. His other hand raised her chin so he could dive into those enormous toffee-colored eyes.

"Stephanie," he whispered, and stood up, bringing her with him.

Her body tightened and she waited, holding her breath. Then, "Michael," and she sank into him, her sweet mouth accepting his, opening for his exploring tongue. Giving him a kiss like those she gave him two years ago. Hot, demanding, giving. All Steph.

How long they stood there, their bodies locked together, their kiss endless, he did not know. He could've stayed forever—until kisses weren't enough. His hands found hers, grasped them to pull her along to his bedroom. "Come with me."

Dear Reader,

Once again I've tackled the subject of infertility, this time from a different perspective. Stephanie Roberts appeared briefly in *The Nurse's Special Delivery* and *Her New Year Baby Surprise*, a duet by me and Louisa George, and I always knew I was going to write her story one day.

When Steph and her husband couldn't conceive through IVF treatment, her life turned upside down. Now, a few years later, she's still struggling to move on, and in steps Michael. Of course, he wants no part of the life she'd love to have, but slowly, slowly, he's drawn in until there's no resisting Steph. I've made it hard for them to get beyond the issues keeping them apart, but in the end the reward makes it all worthwhile.

I hope you enjoy reading *Baby Miracle in the ER*.

All the best,

Sue MacKay

sue.mackay56@yahoo.com

BABY MIRACLE
IN THE ER

SUE MACKAY

HARLEQUIN® MEDICAL ROMANCE™

Recycling programs
for this product may
not exist in your area.

ISBN-13: 978-1-335-66353-5

Baby Miracle in the ER

First North American Publication 2018

Copyright © 2018 by Sue MacKay

Printed in U.S.A.

www.Harlequin.com

Writing is a lonely occupation and yet we as authors cannot do it alone.

Baby Miracle in the ER is the twenty-fifth Harlequin book I have written for the Medical Romance series, and it's dedicated to the people who helped me along the way. Number one, my husband. He has been unfailing in his support through the good and bad times. More dedications to my family, my dearest friends, the Blenheim Writers Group and my writing friends. Thank you all so much for being there for me.

**Praise for
Sue MacKay**

"Ms. MacKay has penned a delightful novel in this book where there were moments where I smiled and moments where I wanted to cry."
—*Harlequin Junkie* on
Resisting Her Army Doc Rival

CHAPTER ONE

'AHHH!' TEARS STREAMED DOWN the pregnant woman's face while fear glared out at paramedic Stephanie Roberts. 'It can't be a contraction!'

No, please not that.

Steph pushed her elbows into her sides to control a shudder. The baby was ten weeks too early, according to the garbled comments the woman's work colleague had uttered as she and Kath, her crew partner, had loaded their patient into the ambulance.

Steph's heart grew heavy as the woman's grip on her hand tightened unbearably. 'Melanie, I want you to breathe deeply and try to stay calm.'

'Stay *calm*? When I'm losing my babies again. Tell me how to *do* that.' Her voice rose on every word until she was practically screaming. 'It's not *fair*.'

I will do everything I possibly can to prevent that outcome.

Using her free hand to wipe her patient's forehead, Steph read the heart monitor. All surprisingly normal there.

'Babies? You're having twins?' That would explain the early contraction. Twins often didn't go the distance *in utero*, but this early was not good.

'Yes!' Melanie huffed. 'We had IVF.' Another huff. 'For the third time.'

That grip on Steph's hand would break something any second now.

It was nothing compared to the ache in Steph's heart, though. Having to undergo IVF in the first place came with a load of unbearable pain and stress. Losing the resultant baby or babies would be beyond description. She herself hadn't got that far, but it had been bad enough—and the consequences even worse. This woman was facing her third round of unbelievable heartbreak if these babies weren't saved.

Stephanie couldn't comprehend that—not even with her own experience of being unable to have children.

'If it's okay, I'm going to examine you. We need to know what's going on.'

Maybe there was some miracle floating around that would mean the pain was just a stomach ache. Not that Steph was into miracles. There hadn't been any going spare when *she'd* needed one, but Melanie might be luckier.

'My back's been aching all morning, my waters broke, and now I've had a contraction. I know what that means.'

The woman's teeth dug so deep into her lip Steph looked for blood. None. *Yet.*

'Except I want to deny it so that it isn't true.'

She doesn't want me confirming what she suspects. I totally get that. But I'm a paramedic, not a counsellor.

Tugging her hand free, Steph moved along the stretcher and gently lifted her patient's skirt and lowered her panties. Dilation had begun. She bit back a curse. They weren't carrying *one* incubator, let alone two.

Now what? These twins had to be saved. They just had to be. *Somehow.*

Tucking the clothing back in place, Steph stepped to the front of the ambulance, where Kath was focusing on the road, and spoke quietly and urgently. 'We haven't got time to go to Auckland Women's. Those babies are intent on making an entrance and I doubt they're going to take their time about it. Head to Auckland Central Hospital as fast as you're allowed.'

Actually, faster than they were allowed—irresponsible or not. But of course Kath wouldn't do that. And nor would Steph if she were behind the wheel. Or perhaps she might, knowing what their patient was facing. The speed limit was there for a good reason, but sometimes rules were made to be broken.

'I'll let Central ED know the situation.' Kath reached for the radio handpiece while simultaneously pressing the accelerator a little harder. 'Sorry I handed you this one.'

Not half as sorry as I am.

'It's fine.' Steph's heart lurched as she returned to their patient. Life could be so horribly cruel. 'Has your husband been told what's happening?'

'Someone at work rang him. He's going to meet us at the hospital.'

'Then we need to let him know where we're taking you. Where's your phone?'

'You just said we're going to Auckland Central, but my specialist said I have to go to National Women's if anything goes wrong.'

Those terrified eyes widened, glittering with unshed tears, and Melanie's chest rose and fell, rose and fell.

'There isn't time. I get it.' The fear became agony. 'Why do we keep trying? Why are we putting ourselves through this when it never goes right for us? What have I ever done to deserve this? I only want a baby. People have them all the time—easy.'

Steph reached for her hand, let Melanie hold tight; too bad if her metatarsals were fractured. Apart from taking obs and willing the ambulance to go faster there wasn't much else she could do. She certainly couldn't soften the truth;

because she pretty much knew what her patient was going through.

'Please don't do this to yourself.'

As if the woman could stop.

If the outcome wasn't good, those questions would haunt Melanie for months, even years to come. But Steph would make sure that didn't happen. There was no room for things going wrong. Not this time—not today.

'Concentrate on breathing normally so you're not agitating your babies. I know it's hard, but we have to try.'

'You think *breathing* is going to save my babies?'

The eye-roll didn't quite come off but hurt still stabbed Steph under the ribs.

Because she couldn't save the babies if they persisted in coming out into the world before reaching the emergency department. That would take a team of gynaecologists and neonatal specialists and a room full of specialised equipment and—oh, look, none of those were on board right now.

And because... *Yeah, well.* Because some things were never forgotten. No matter how hard she tried, how much she turned her life upside down and all around, Steph understood some of this woman's anguish too well.

'Mark's going to be devastated.' Melanie gulped.

Concentrate.

'Your husband?' she asked softly around the lump of sadness building in her throat. Sadness for Melanie or herself? Both?

'Yes.'

'Want me to call him?'

Someone had to let him know their new destination and that his wife was struggling at the moment. Not that Steph wanted to be the one to break his heart, but it seemed he was a stayer— had hung around after the first time this had happened. And the second. Chances were he'd do the same again. Melanie mightn't understand but there was *some* luck on her side.

'Would you?' Melanie tapped her screen and handed the phone over, her teeth nibbling at her lip.

Right, get this done. Tap the phone icon, listen to the ringing, ignore the thumping in your chest. Get it finished, then focus on making this ride as comfortable as possible.

Kind of impossible, given the circumstances, but she'd do all she could to—

'Ahhh!' Her patient's hands clenched and strain tightened her face.

'Don't push, whatever you do.'

Easy said...

Shoving the phone aside, Steph moved to re-examine the woman's cervix. And cursed under her breath. These babies had an agenda of their own and no one, especially their mother, was about to deflect them. What if the babies popped out before they arrived at the hospital? What could she do to keep their chances of survival alive?

Think, girl, think.

The CPAP for breathing. Blankets for warmth. She could only hope they'd get to ED before any of that was needed.

Another contraction was tightening Melanie's belly. 'I can't do this.'

'We're doing it together.' Steph reached for a chilled hand, squeezed gently before once again examining her patient—and not liking what she was seeing.

Straightening up, she reached for the nitrous oxide. 'Suck on that next time you have a contraction.'

'I'm such a failure.'

'Hey, don't beat yourself up. Right now we've got two babies to think about and how best to increase their chances. So, are you up to sucking on that gas when required?'

A sharp nod.

Steph didn't have time for any more chit-chat. The baby that had been crowning when she'd last looked was now about to slip out into the world.

Preparing for the birth by strategically placing the Continuous Positive Airway Pressure instrument nearby, and soft, light blankets ready to receive the precious bundle, she held her breath and watched and waited for the inevitable.

The blue of her gloves was a sharp contrast to the pale skin on Melanie's thighs. It seemed impersonal to be welcoming a newborn into the world with a pair of vinyl-covered hands, but it was safer, and this little tot would need all the protection from infections and bugs it was humanly possible to achieve. It had to survive, and survive well.

Melanie tensed. 'Here we go again,' she forced out through gritted teeth.

'You're doing fine.'

No point telling her otherwise. Baby was coming, ready or not. *OMG*. So tiny and vulnerable. And blue.

Steph worked fast but carefully, knew nothing but that she was trying to save the tiniest boy she'd ever laid eyes upon.

Why hadn't she trained as a paediatrician instead of a nurse?

A tap on her shoulder didn't stop her.

'We've got this.' A male command. 'Fill me in fast.'

A quick sideways glance showed a man in scrubs. A further look around and she gasped with relief. The ambulance had stopped, the doors were open and emergency staff were crowding in.

'First baby arrived…' she glanced at her watch

'...three minutes ago. There's another coming. They're ten weeks early.'

She rattled off details and obs, handing over the baby to another scrubbed-up doctor, who immediately began working on the infant.

Suddenly she was redundant. That relief expanded. Those babies weren't relying on her and now had a fighting chance. Fingers crossed. She'd given her all, but was it enough?

Squeezing through to the front of the ambulance to avoid the crowd of medical staff at the rear, she hopped out through Kath's door and stood out of the way, watching as the experts delivered the second baby. At least this wee lad went straight into an incubator. The first baby had already disappeared amidst gowned, masked staff with one purpose in their minds—to save his life.

Steph's chest ached where her heart thumped. These babies *had* to make it. No other outcome was acceptable.

'Can you unload the stretcher for us?' someone asked.

Instantly Steph was at the back of the ambulance, unlocking the wheels as Kath took the weight to roll the stretcher out.

'Here we go,' she warned Melanie, who was looking all hollowed out, her face sunken, her eyes glittering with tears, hands limp on her less rotund stomach.

'Are they—?'

'Yes,' Kath said firmly.

Please, please live, Steph begged the babies. *Your mum needs you.*

Once Melanie had been transferred to a bed Steph leaned close. 'I'll be thinking about you. Hang in there and all the best.'

Then she made herself scarce, not looking around the department where she'd worked until two years ago, not wanting those memories on top of what had gone down today.

Her knees were wobbly. Her head thumped. And, damn it, her eyes were tearing up. Quite the professional.

Around the corner, out of everyone's way and sight, Stephanie stopped to lean her forehead against the cold wall and clasped her hands together on top of her head, her eyes squeezed shut in an attempt to halt the threatening waterfall.

Her first day working as a paramedic in Auckland and history had slapped her around the head. Her one attempt at IVF five years ago had failed and her husband had refused to try again, saying it was a waste of time when the doctors couldn't find any reason for her infertility.

No problems in *his* department, apparently. And no relief for her empty arms that longed to hold her own baby. It had hit her hard today. Much harsher than it had in a while. She guessed that was what happened when she returned home to where it had all happened.

'Stephanie? Is that you?'

The deep, throaty voice spun her name into unwelcome heated memories and warmed her skin to knock sideways the chill that had taken over in the ambulance.

Michael. Don't move.

It might be that she'd imagined him. Anything was possible today.

'Hello,' he said. 'Welcome back. You've been missed around here.'

The air swirled around her, touching down on the exposed skin of her face, her neck, her hands. A shape lined up beside her. A peek to the right and there was no doubt about it. Her imagination had *not* been playing games. She wasn't sure if that was good. Or bad.

Dr Michael Laing's shoulders and back rested against the wall, those legs that went on for ever were crossed at the ankles and his hands—oh, yeah, she remembered those hands as much as his lips—were jammed into the pockets of his crumpled scrubs. Just as she remembered him— utterly gorgeous, with that never quite styled hair falling over his forehead in soft curls.

When he said, 'Still as quiet as ever,' she shivered.

She wasn't ready for this—not after those babies arriving in her unprepared hands. 'Hi.'

Now leave me to pull myself together.

Right then her nose ran and she had to sniff.

He dug into a back pocket, held a handkerchief out. 'Here, use this. I promise it's clean.'

Did he have to sound *exactly* the same? Couldn't he have grown a polyp in his throat? Or permanently lost his voice from too much shouting at the sidelines of a rugby game?

'Those babies got to you, didn't they? They would have got me too if I'd been there. Stephanie…' He paused, gentled his voice. 'They're in expert hands, and everyone in PICU will be working their butts off to save them.'

Pushing away from the wall, she eyeballed him. Nearly choked on a sudden inhalation of air. *Michael.* That open, friendly face, those intense azure eyes still with the thin layer of need he'd hate to be recognised, that tempting mouth…

'I know. Sorry for being a goof.'

'Hardly. You're human.'

His smile was warm. Tentative?

She blew her nose, gave herself breathing space. 'I'm fine. Really.'

I was until twenty seconds ago. Liar.

She hadn't been right since she realised her patient's IVF babies were coming far too early.

His gaze was caring. Oh, how she remembered that caring. It was his middle name.

'My thoughts exactly. Just having a bit of a

kip against the wall. I get it. It's how I cope with a crisis too.'

Uh-uh. Not so. Her memory was excellent. This man dealt with harrowing issues by striding out for hours, those long legs chewing up kilometre after kilometre as he went over and over whatever was eating him up. Her leg muscles had ached for days after she'd stuck with him for nearly three hours, charging along the city waterfront, listening as he worked his way through grief and anger one particularly dark day.

'I haven't suffered a crisis.'

Not much.

So why were her knees feeling like over-oiled hinges?

His mouth quirked in a funny, heart-slowing way. 'You used to be embarrassingly honest.'

As in, *I feel something for you, Michael and would love to continue seeing you*, honest?

But unlike that day, when he'd intoned in a flat voice that he wasn't interested, now there was a friendly warmth in his voice that touched her deeply. Made her feel vulnerable as the longing to tell him everything cascaded through her.

Tightening her knees, lifting her chin, stuffing that need way down in a dark place, she went with a different truth. 'I'm gutted that I couldn't stop those babies coming.' Even though she was not a doctor. 'They're far too early.'

His elbow nudged her lightly. 'No one would've

been able to do that, Stephanie. Please stop beating yourself up. You don't deserve it.'

Seemed he cared that she got this right—which, if she wasn't prudent, could make falling into those eyes too easy, could make leaving today behind for a while effortless.

Some of the frost that had been enveloping her heart for so long melted. 'That doesn't stop me wishing I could've.'

His eyes lightened as he looked her over with that smile lingering at the corners of his mouth, offering her support when she most definitely hadn't asked for it. Not that she didn't want to ask, but laying her heart out for him to see when she was messed up over those babies would not be her greatest move.

Time to go back to base and hopefully a straightforward call-out to someone who thought they were having a heart attack but in reality had indigestion. Whoever it was would get all the care Steph was capable of before being handed over to the ED staff. And at least then she wouldn't feel as though the ground had been cut from under her.

'Kath's full of praise for you. Says you were awesome.' Michael held her gaze. 'Hold on to that thought. Stop punishing yourself. It's not your fault your patient was well on the way to going into full labour by the time you picked her up. There wasn't another thing you could've done.'

Ping. Her lips lifted of their own volition. 'Back at me, huh?'

Her words of wisdom from years ago weren't so easy to accept when they came from the opposite direction.

'Only because you were right.'

He hadn't thought so at the time—had said she didn't know what she was talking about, didn't understand his grief over losing that little boy.

'Being a paramedic seems harder because the buck stops with us until we get to an emergency department. I never felt alone when I was working in here, or so responsible for someone else.'

So gutted when the situation turned to custard. The odds on one, let alone both those babies surviving were long. A shudder rocked her and she wrapped her arms around herself.

'Yet even in here you fought tooth and nail for your patients, no matter who else was around.'

His words were a balm, a gentle caress of understanding, and she needed that.

Steph wrestled with the urge to lean in against that expansive chest, tightening her hands into fists, rocking on her toes, flattening her mouth, staying away.

This was Michael—the man she'd worked with, laughed and joked with, shared one intense night with while they'd walked and talked for hours about a wee boy who'd died under his care. A night that had ended in making love for hours and which had led to more nights of wonder until—*ping!*—it was over. Gone in a quiet conversation about responsibilities and life and not getting involved.

He was one of the reasons she'd scarpered out of town and away from the job she'd loved, leaving her family and friends, renting out her house, to head to Queenstown where she knew no one. *One* of the reasons. Another of those reasons had also raised its sorry head today. Obviously a day for reliving the past. Great—just when she was starting over. *Again.*

There'd been a lot of starting over during the last two years. Which might explain this sinking sadness pulling at her. As if she was being tested to see if this was what she really wanted.

Yes, she did. As she had every other move. And every time the excitement and certainty had run its course and left her confused and a little more lost. But this time she was back home where she belonged for good. This was where her family was, her best friend, her past: the good and the ugly. It *had* to work out or she had no idea what else to do with herself. She had to accept once and for all that she would never have her own baby.

'Ready to go, Steph?' Kath appeared in her line of sight.

'More than.' She almost choked on the words. The need to be busy doing something—anything—was beginning to suffocate her. 'Good to see you again, Michael.'

She acknowledged the man beside her, ignored the disappointment filling his eyes, and headed to the ambulance bay without a backward glance. The only safe way to go. She'd got that first meeting out of the way—now she could move forward, box ticked. But first she needed to pull herself together and look the part of a happy woman tearing through life like there was no tomorrow.

Michael stared after Stephanie, absorbing the protectiveness he'd felt for her the moment he'd laid eyes on her, wanting to banish whatever had caused all that hurting going on, knowing he couldn't unless he was prepared to let her close.

Stephanie Roberts really was back in town. Rumour had warned him—reality frightened him. He'd been prepared as much as possible to see her, had been ready to say *Hi, how's things?* and get on with his day. He hadn't been expecting the slam of recognition from his body at the sight of her, the intense longing for her to be at his side, with him throughout…*everything*.

What he wanted now was to wipe away that pain, bring on a smile full of warmth—not that tight *I-am-not-hiding-anything* grimace that actually hid nothing. Forget staying uninvolved. At least until she was smiling again.

What's wrong, Steph? What happened to throw you against that wall like you couldn't stand up by yourself?

He knew her as a strong woman who didn't buckle easily. Or so he'd believed. Something had undermined that strength today.

His jaw clenched. Tension rippled through his muscles. Did her mouth still tip up higher on the left side when she gave a genuine, big-hearted smile? He'd thought he'd conquered those sweet memories of how he wanted to sing and dance when she smiled. Of how her toffee eyes were easier to read than a toddler's book. Of how calm he felt around her.

She'd never asked anything of him—except to go to a football match with her which, when interpreted, had meant have a future together. That had scared the pants off him and had had him hauling on the brakes fast. Getting in too deep hadn't been an option. He hadn't been able to give her the certainty she deserved, the 'for ever' she wanted.

Yet five minutes standing beside her, worrying about what was wrong, and it was as though the mantra he lived by had vamoosed.

He shook his hands, flexed his fingers, worked the tension out of his gut. There hadn't been a lot of ease between him and Stephanie just now. Nor a lot of smiling. Stephanie's eyes, laden with sadness—or was that despair?—and the colour draining from her cheeks had been like a rugby tackle around his knees.

Had she made the wrong choice when she'd swapped scrubs for a paramedic's uniform and that was what was getting to her? No, there was depth to that sadness—close to deep pain. That didn't come from changing jobs…not even for dedicated Stephanie.

Why aren't you back here working with me, Stephanie? Us? When did you cut off all that long, thick blonde hair?

'How've you been? *Really?*' he asked her shadow as she turned the corner into the ambulance bay.

He'd missed her.

Not that he was admitting it. No way in hell.

A recollection of gremlins haunting her on bad days nagged at him. Shame he couldn't recall the story of what had gone down in her life before he'd joined the department. He had an aversion to rumours and liked facts. And today the key to all this was there, swinging just out of reach. To catch it he had to follow up on today and track her down for a catch-up.

Or he could wait, since they'd be bumping into each regularly if she was operating out of the local St John base. So, no catch-up needed— which meant he could dodge a bullet.

They'd worked well together, had been friendly, and apart from those intoxicating two weeks had had little to do with each other out-side of the ED. Best it was left like that. She'd handed in her notice a fortnight after they'd split and he'd felt uneasy ever since. As though he'd lost the one chance of real happiness he'd had because he hadn't been prepared to put the past behind him and take a stand.

'Shouldn't you be knocking off?' James, head of the next shift, nudged him. 'Unless you've got nothing better to do than hang around staring after Stephanie Roberts—which surprises me.'

Why? Any man with blood in his veins would be doing the same—which kind of said James had ink in his. Something to be grateful for.

'I'm on my way.'

Not that he had anything planned for the night. Doing his washing didn't count, and getting some groceries would take care of all of twenty minutes. Both his close mates were tied up with babies and wives and apparent domestic bliss. Lucky guys.

It's all yours for the taking if you want it.

He didn't. One divorce was one too many on his life CV. Besides, there were already more than enough complications going down outside of work that left no time for him to care about anyone else. *But*...

The word was drawn out. But sometimes he wished he was going home to someone special—

someone to love and be loved by with no quali-
fication. Instantly Stephanie came to mind.

Jerking his head up, he snapped at James,
'Have a busy night. Catch you tomorrow.'

Immediately he felt a heel. If this was what
briefly seeing Stephanie did then he couldn't
manage spending any more time with her. He'd
be a wreck within hours.

Charging through the department to his locker
as if he had the ball and was being chased by
the opposition forward pack, he snatched up his
jacket and the keys to his motorbike. A spin over
the harbour bridge in the chill winter air might
cool his brain and freeze Stephanie out. And if
it didn't? Then he was in for a long night.

Once upon a time Monday nights meant
drinks with the guys after rugby practice at the
clubroom. Now it tended to be pizza delivery
and catching up on emails and other scintillat-
ing stuff at home. Of course he got an earful of
noise from his mates for being the only one still
single. Jock and Max could never leave him to
get on with his perfectly ordered life. They loved
getting in his face about it too much.

The idea of pizza didn't excite him today.
Truth? It had stopped being exciting after the
fourth Monday in a row—about two years
back. But he wasn't being picky if the alternative meant cooking something. Though the steak

in his fridge *would* make a tasty change… *Nah.* Then there'd be dishes to do.

'I see Steph's become a paramedic.'

James was still with him, digging into his locker as well, apparently in the mood for talking.

'Wonder why she's gone to the other side?'

Michael hoped it wasn't because she couldn't work with him any more. But that was more likely his ego getting in the way of common sense. Whatever the reason, he should be glad she hadn't returned to this department as a nurse, despite his wishing she had.

Working together was not an option when she tipped him off his pedestal too easily.

'Crewing ambulances isn't too far removed from the emergency department. Still the same patients, the same urgency and caring.'

The same sadness when something went belly-up. Could it just be that she was insecure about her ability? He wasn't accepting that. Not from Stephanie Roberts.

'But she was *made* to be an ED nurse.' James looked puzzled. 'Then again, we haven't seen her in a while, so who knows what's gone down in her life recently?'

Nothing awful, he hoped.

'She's not the first to take a change in vocation. There are days I wish I'd stuck to my rugby career, though my body is eternally grateful I didn't.'

His half-sisters hadn't been so thrilled at the change either, when it had dawned on them that he had less time and money to sort their problems.

'You were good enough for a full-time career?'

The stunned look on James's face had Michael laughing—and swallowing an unexpected mouthful of nostalgia.

'You'd better believe it. I played franchise rugby for over two years. I was out on the wing until a heavy knock resulting in a second moderate concussion had me thinking that if I wanted to be a doctor after the rugby inevitably came to an end then I needed to look out for my brain. So I handed in my boots.'

He hadn't been able to afford the risk of not having all his faculties in working order when he'd had other responsibilities needing his undivided attention. His half-sisters were his priority—had been since the day his father had extracted his promise to be the man around the place and look after them and their mother when he was thirteen, and from the way things were going, always would be.

Chantelle, in particular, made big enough messes with her life. What she'd have done if anything had happened to him was anyone's guess. One that he no longer thought about. Instead he'd just accepted his role to be there for both of them continuously, to save them whenever things went wrong—as they did far too often with Chantelle. Thankfully Carly seemed settled in her new life in England. Strange how she'd managed to sort herself out once he hadn't been there to support her… Their mother had taken off overseas so there was no having her to sort out.

'No regrets?'

He didn't need this conversation, but he'd been short with James and wanted to negate anything bad.

'Some—but there'd have been a lot more if I'd suffered serious head injuries.' Playing such a physical sport always had its issues. 'Quitting was the right call.'

At first he'd missed the team camaraderie and the thrill of winning a hard-fought-for game, but he still had his two closest mates and it hadn't taken him long to get into his stride studying to become a doctor. He'd had plenty of practice helping his half-sisters out of the mischief and chaos they'd got into, so extending that help into a medical career where he dealt with vulnerable people daily—hourly—was natural. Which was why losing a patient despite giving everything he had in the tank always hurt.

Stephanie's earlier sadness had twisted his

gut. She'd know those babies would now be tucked into incubators with monitors attached to their tiny bodies while specialists worked their butts off to save them. Yet he suspected she still needed a shoulder to cry on, or a friend to walk it out with, talk it through with—except, being her, there probably wouldn't be much talking.

What time did her shift finish?

Leave it alone. Stay uninvolved.

But he owed her. She'd been there for him when Jacob Brown had died in his hands. She'd listened without lecturing, she'd walked beside him as he dashed around the city for hours and had limped for days afterwards. She'd kissed him to the point when he didn't know where he began and ended. She'd fallen into his bed as eagerly as he'd taken her there.

Definitely stay away.

It had been two years. She wouldn't be the same woman. Must have another man in her life, in her bed by now.

Anger flared.

Down, boy. You have no rights here. You sent her packing.

If there *was* someone special he should be pleased. She'd be able to talk out what was bothering her tonight.

The anger only increased, and he felt his hands clenched at his sides, his abs drawn tight.

Go—ride over the bridge, head north for an hour. Turn off the brain. Then order pizza.

Man or no man in her life, Stephanie had family and friends here. He knew that much from the past. She'd be fine. Better off if it wasn't *him* hanging around like a dog after a bone. He might make a mistake and touch her again. He still burned with the need to hug her that had floored him the moment he'd first seen her pressed up against the wall as though she could no longer hold herself together.

Hell. He had not given her what she needed. He'd let her go without a word. Without a hug. Without an honest-to-goodness *Glad to see you and I want to help you* smile. Just like last time.

Wise move for him.

Unkind and unfair on her.

CHAPTER TWO

STEPH SLIPPED INTO her jacket with a grateful sigh. The ambulance was restocked for the night crew. Six o'clock had clicked over on her watch. Definitely time to be someplace else.

Only that meant picking up something from the supermarket to take back to the house to heat and eat while watching the second instalment of the thriller she'd recorded last weekend.

A night on her own wasn't appealing after the day she'd had. If only her brother and Jill weren't away on their extended honeymoon she'd go and hassle them and talk about random stuff that had nothing to do with babies or Michael.

For a moment her mood lightened. She still struggled to get her head around her brother marrying her best friend. Their relationship was grounded in history and love. A *lot* of love.

Stepping outside, she gasped as cold, damp air dumped on her. The Italian summer she'd enjoyed last month seemed for ever ago. The zip on her jacket pinched her chin when she tugged it high. When had this drizzle started? It had been dry on their last call-out—but then it *had* been dark and she hadn't been weather-watching.

'Hi, Stephanie.'

Only one person called her Stephanie. Usually she didn't like it, thought it too formal, but in that particular deep, husky voice it was more than okay. Or was that only because she was feeling so out of whack?

'Michael.'

'You're done for the day?'

'Yes, thank goodness.'

The need to be busy had long disappeared, leaving her drained and despondent. Glancing around the car park she saw him standing at the open driver's door of a shiny hatchback—nothing like what she'd expected him to be driving. Too domestic. Did he still own a motorbike?

'It's been a long day.'

That was telling him too much. From deep inside, she dredged up a smile, denied the tightness those long legs and toned thighs filling his jeans created in her toes.

'Have you been loitering around the ambulance station?'

'Yep.' He grinned cheekily. 'I tried walking in but this place is like a fort.'

'We can't let in just *anyone*—especially doctors with nothing better to do with their time.'

What was Michael doing here? Surely he hadn't stopped by to say hello to *her*?

'Not sure if you know, but those babies are hanging in there, doing as well as can be expected. I phoned PICU as I was leaving for the day.'

He'd come to tell her that? Seriously? Mr Non-Involved had found out the most important news for her.

'No one would tell me a thing because I'm not related. I was desperate to know how they were doing.' *Careful.* 'That's fantastic.' Definitely better than the alternative.

'There are *some* advantages with my position.'

His grin was now a soft smile, winding around her like a cloud of kindness.

'Want some company for a bit? Talk some? Up to you.'

Amazement stopped her feet from moving forward, stalled her brain. He'd offered *that* to the woman he'd once told he didn't want anything more to do with outside of work? The man was still single. Or so she'd heard from one of the ED nurses. Not that she'd been asking...

Come on. He's hot, popular and fun. There's single, and then there's single with a woman on his arm.

There'd always been a queue of women waiting for his attention. Gorgeous young women who could have babies. Not a thirty-two-year-old

with a chip on her shoulder bigger than the cra-
ter on Mount Ruapehu, who hadn't been able to
conceive with her ex no matter how often they'd
tried.

*You promised to leave all this behind and
start over when you returned home. One bad
day doesn't give you reason to go back on that.*

Yeah, yeah.

'I'll take a rain-check.'

Wimp.

'I need to get out of my uniform, then eat
something.' Now that her stomach had settled
down to normal it was hinting that grub would
be good.

'If food's what you're wanting it's pizza night.'

He wasn't begging, nor pushing too hard. He
was saying she was welcome to share a meal if
she wanted. And talk if she needed.

That was *not* happening.

'Pizza night? Because it's Monday?'

Michael nodded and gave a wry smile. 'Tues-
day's Thai.'

Steph couldn't help it. She laughed. So much
for keeping her distance. 'Cooking not your
thing?'

'Always seems a bit pointless when it's only
for me.'

'I can relate to that.' Definitely still single.

He locked his eyes on her. 'Well? Join me? You

can jump in and I'll call you a cab when you're ready to go home.'

She hesitated. It was so tempting.

Oh, get real. You came home to face up to Michael, work him out of your system once and for ever. So start now.

While one half of her brain was raving the other side thought spending some downtime with this man might not be the wisest thing to do. Especially tonight, when her emotions were already ragged.

'My car's right here.'

The sporty little number had been her big indulgence the day she'd arrived back in town. All part of the statement she'd made about settling down for good. Every time she climbed into the car it was a reminder of that. Some days it made her happy. Today she wasn't so sure she'd done the right thing.

'Then follow me.'

She hadn't forgotten where he lived. How could she with all those memories of what they'd got up to in his house?

Opening his car door, he paused. 'I'm not going to pressure you into talking about something you'd prefer not to, Stephanie. Chilling out after something that obviously upset you today could be cathartic. That's all.'

He was offering to do for her what she'd done for him when he'd been cut up over losing that little boy. Her chest squeezed painfully. Why not? He would do that for anyone, because he knew what they'd be feeling, thinking, wanting.

Anyone, Steph, not just you.

Which was why she answered with, 'I'll be right behind you.'

She could always take a wrong turn if she changed her mind in the next few minutes.

Except the pull of hot food that she didn't have to prepare—meaning throw in the microwave—was hard to ignore. Her empty house would be cold. More than that, the idea of company for an hour or two was impossible to refuse. Especially Michael's company.

A car turned into the parking lot, its head-lights swishing across Michael's car, showing what she'd been too busy focusing on him to notice. In the back was a child's car seat with a small child strapped in to it—which explained the family wagon.

Was that why Michael had aborted their fling back when she'd fallen for him? He'd already had a woman in his life? The mother of his child?

Her stomach clenched. But he'd said no commitment and claimed he was happy on his own. Interesting. Confusing. And the end to the idea of sharing pizza.

'Sorry—change of plan. I think you've already got enough people in your life without adding *me* to the mix.'

A frown appeared. Then he saw the direction her eyes had taken. 'You haven't met Aaron yet.'

'Very smart of you.'

It could be Michael Junior, for all she cared. She wasn't getting caught up in anything that involved another woman in his life—not even for some cathartic relaxation.

'Best I head away.'

His sigh carried across the wet concrete. 'Aaron's my nephew. I've just picked him up from daycare. We often hang out together in my house when I'm not at work. We'd love some company.' He stopped, his body more tense than it had been a moment ago. 'Okay, *I'd* like *your* company.'

He sure knew how to ramp up the pressure.

Or was it that she didn't know how to resist those friendly eyes filled with concern for her? Could it be that Michael was not quite as confident with women as he made himself out to be? Or was that just with her?

He hadn't often taken advantage of that queue of willing women, she recalled. Then again, it had been a while since she'd seen him and anything could have happened to change him.

Stop overthinking things.

What harm would a couple of hours' eating and chatting cause? It wasn't as though she was signing up for life. No, she was *getting over* him for life.

'Lead on.'

Her heart was safe, she assured herself. He'd already rejected her and they wouldn't be going back over old ground.

Her sigh was long and slow. Getting over him had seemed straightforward when she'd left Auckland. She wasn't falling for that trick this time. It was going to take time and patience and toughness—starting with spending time with him.

'Bugsy's gone!' Aaron hollered at the top of his lungs.

How could such a small body create so much noise?

'We're nearly home, buddy. I'll get him for you then.' Michael took a quick look in the rearview mirror at the following headlights. Stephanie?

A streetlight shone on the red paintwork of the racy little number that she drove. Surprise lifted his mood. Gave him a warm, fuzzy moment. As if he needed a woman's attention…

Stephanie isn't just any woman.

Therein lay his problem. He helped others—did not expect the same in return. When he'd promised his father to look out for his half-sisters he'd believed his dad would love him more. *Wrong.* His father loved each of them—but not enough to stay around.

Likewise his ex-wife. She'd told him he'd failed her, hadn't lived up to the promises he'd

made on their wedding day. He still didn't understand that—unless she'd meant he hadn't been
supposed to change careers and move away from
the fame and glamour of rugby to a set of ugly
scrubs.

'I want Bugsy *now*!'

Ouch. His ears hurt. It used to be better when
Aaron couldn't talk.

'Quieten down, buddy. I can't reach him while
I'm driving so you'll have to wait.'

Reasoning with this lad was pointless, but he
kept trying day in, day out, in the hope that eventually Aaron would start to understand that not
everything would go his way all the time. Not
that it helped when his half-sister immediately
undid all his work by spoiling the kid rotten.
It should be *his* role as uncle to spoil him, but
someone had to be the sensible one in this family
and it seemed the cap was made for him.

'Bugsy! Bugsy! Bugsy!'

It would have been funny if the stuffed monkey's name hadn't got louder with each utterance
and tiny feet hadn't been pummelling the back
of Michael's seat.

He chose to ignore the outburst. They usually didn't last long, and tonight he wasn't in
the mood for an argument that would go nowhere. Tonight he wanted to indulge himself for
a change. To allow some 'me' time with Stephanie. Not that he intended anything more than

catching up on what she'd been up to since heading to Queenstown—and maybe learning why
she was now a paramedic and not doing the job
she'd loved so much.

Turning into his wide drive, he held his breath.
Released it when her car pulled up beside his.
She hadn't done a bunk. Which probably meant
she was more upset than she realised.

He was under no illusions that she *wanted* to
spend time talking about those babies and how
lucky they'd been so far. But why had she been
so distressed? He'd seen her deal with losing patients, young and old. Once he'd had to pull her
away from giving CPR when there had been no
chance of bringing their patient back to life. Yet
he'd never seen that level of despair and pain in
her eyes.

'Bugsy!' A solid kick in the back of his seat.

'Aaron, that's enough. We're home now, and
we've got a visitor. A nice lady you can say hello
to.'

Lifting his nephew out of the seat, he had to
hold tight as Aaron wriggled around to see who
this stranger was. The lad loved people—knew
no fear about approaching anyone. Only a good
thing if the world was full of kind souls.

Stephanie flipped her key-lock and joined
them, those slim legs and just right breasts filling her green and black uniform in ways the

designers wouldn't have planned on. Her gaze trolled the front of his massive house.

'I'd forgotten how grand this place is. You did well getting your hands on it.'

Forget *hands*. It had taken a load of hard-earned money, and then some, but it had been worth every cent. Pride filled his chest. It was a very special house—one that had sucked him in the moment he'd seen it from this very spot. It was tucked neatly into a gentle slope, making the most of its location, while inside the floor-to-ceiling windows highlighted the view over Waitemata Harbour, and the deck was the best place in the world to sit and relax after an arduous day in the department.

'I bought it when I quit rugby and began studying full-time. Figured it would be a good investment and there'd be no temptation to fritter away my money over the years until I started earning again.'

'You played professionally—I remember. Why give up?'

Her gaze left the house to cruise his shoulders and chest, headed lower. To his thighs.

At least that was where he presumed her intense gaze was now fixed. Even if it was the concrete he stood on, his groin had tightened anyway. He cursed silently.

For the second time that day he explained. 'Rugby wasn't a career that'd take me into old age.'

The left side of her mouth lifted. His belly joined in on the tightening act.

'Can I carry anything?' she asked as he juggled Aaron and the bag of necessities that went everywhere his nephew did.

'I've got it.'

'You're a dab hand at this,' Steph quipped as he managed to unlock the front door and not drop child or bag. 'Had lots of practice?'

There was more to that question than the obvious. 'Only with this guy.'

That should stop any ideas she might be getting about him and any kids he might have.

The wind rustled the bushes and the drizzle got wetter. 'Come inside before it starts bucketing down.'

'I want Bugsy!' Aaron cried.

Oh, hell.

When he should have been retrieving the toy he'd been focused on watching Stephanie clamber out of her car, noting those legs he had X-rated memories of and that perfectly rounded butt.

'Bugsy!'

'Hang on, buddy. I'll get him in a minute.' First he had to unload onto the entrance table.

'Something I can do?'

'There's a stuffed monkey in the back of my car. Under my seat, I think.'

'I'll grab it.'

'Thanks.'

Car tyres squealed on his driveway. *Chantelle*. And in a foul mood, judging by the flat mouth and glittering eyes. Stephanie was about to learn more about his private life than she'd ever wanted to know.

'Michael, when are you going to stop interfering in my life?'

'Mummy!' Aaron wriggled out of his arms and trotted to Chantelle.

'Hey, baby.' Chantelle might be angry with him, but there was only love in her eyes when she swung her boy up into her arms. 'How's my darling?'

'Chantelle, I want you to meet—'

The love dipped as she yelled, 'I didn't ask you to pick him up. So I'll say it again. When are you going to stop interfering in my life?'

When you stop expecting me to... When you stand on your own two feet all the time.

'They phoned from the daycare centre to say you hadn't turned up and they couldn't get hold of you.'

He held on to his own temper, knowing from experience that losing it wouldn't help a thing— especially when Chantelle was in one of her rages. A quick glance across to Stephanie and his stomach curdled at her shocked expression.

'Chantelle, can we—?'

'That doesn't mean you can charge in and take

over. I got there before they closed. That's all that matters,' Chantelle ranted.

No mystery about where Aaron got his lungs from.

Michael closed his eyes, dug deep for composure—because right about now he was going to lose it, and that couldn't happen. What sort of example would that set for Aaron? Plus, he most definitely did *not* want Stephanie seeing him getting angry.

'Mike, you've got to stop taking charge all the time.'

The octave levels had dropped, and Chantelle was using 'Mike', meaning he was in for a lecture.

She began placing Aaron in the car seat in her own vehicle. 'I'm a good mum. You've said so yourself. I hadn't forgotten Aaron—I just got caught up with a tutor going over my last paper and time got away. It happens—and not just to me.' She stabbed the car's rooftop with a finger. 'I never forgot about him, and I knew I had to get to the centre before six-thirty.'

He lived with the dread that his beautiful sister would start the slippery slide back into hell and this time take his nephew with her. But she had a point. She was an excellent mother and she didn't neglect Aaron—she loved him to bits.

'I'm sorry.'

'Yeah, yeah.'

The door slammed, and then she was belting herself into her seat and revving the engine. At least she had the sense to back out slowly, and her speed down the drive was careful. Just as it should be with a three-year-old on board.

Stephanie stared after the car as the tail-lights disappeared out of sight. 'What just happened?'

'You haven't met my sister.'

Her eyes widened as she turned to look at him. 'That was your *sister*?' Disbelief echoed between them.

'We're not alike.' *At all.* Same father—nothing much else to show a connection. Though that wasn't true. They had the same colouring. The same wariness. Had learnt the hard way about sharing themselves with outsiders.

'You okay that you're not getting time with your nephew?'

'I'm good. I'd better order that pizza.'

He didn't move, suddenly exhausted. Watching out for his sister did that to him sometimes. He needed time out. Strange, but he knew Chantelle would be the first to tell him to go for it.

Stephanie was making him uncomfortable with her intense scrutiny. 'I'll take a rain-check. You look like you could do with some alone time.'

'Can't say I'm hungry any more. Sorry.'

Her hand gripped his arm. 'Michael, it's fine. Truly. We can catch up another time.'

'Thanks for understanding.'

'Who says I did?'

Her smile kicked him in the gut.

'See you tomorrow.'

Steph slid into her car, clicked the belt in place, watching Michael standing there, waiting patiently for her to leave. *Wanting* her to leave.

Would he phone his sister and have it out with her? Or did this happen often enough that he'd let it wash over him? He didn't look comfortable—had been tense from the moment that car had flown up the drive and Chantelle had leapt out. Talk about a human tornado…

Putting the gear in reverse, she started to back away. Hunger pangs hit her. The idea of something nuked made her wince. It wasn't the way to look after herself. Was there a restaurant on the way home that'd do a takeaway for her?

Something banged lightly on her window. She braked and Michael appeared at her door.

'Come inside. I invited you here and now I'm letting you go without feeding you.'

If she went inside with him his sister's accusations would follow them, hold them back from relaxing over easy conversation.

'Not tonight.'

But they both needed to eat. An idea struck.

'Get in. We'll go for a beer and a meal at the pub round the corner.'

He'd say no. But the idea of sitting in a warm pub with lots of people to distract her was brilliant.

'I'm headed there.'

'I'm supposed to squeeze into this tiny thing you call a car?'

Turning her down was warring with interest in his eyes.

'See it as a challenge.'

He never dodged one of those.

The passenger door opened.

'My knees and ears are about to become best mates.'

She laughed. 'Do you want to tip the seat back so you can lie down?'

Finally the last of the ball of tension in her stomach unravelled and she played the piano on the steering wheel until Michael got belted in. Spending time with him was exactly what she needed—not her empty, lonely house.

At the pub, with drinks in hand and fish and chips ordered, they found somewhere to sit away from the noise of people talking too loudly. It was good to get a load off her feet and lean back against the leather-covered wall of the booth.

'Just what the doctor ordered.' She sipped her beer.

Michael mimicked her. 'Perfect.'

After glancing around the crowded room he came back to look at her.

'Tell me about Queenstown. There's so much to do outdoors—what did you try?'

Staying on safe subjects was good. 'I learned to ski—or rather I started to. Falling off and twisting my ankle put me off *that* pursuit. Next I joined a tramping club and went on some amazing walks in the mountains—until a group of us had to sleep outside an overcrowded hut one night. Being woken by a huge possum crawling over my sleeping bag gave me the heebie-jeebies and I quit tramping.' She shuddered. 'Furry creepy beasts...coming right up to my head looking for food.'

'Then you took up crochet?'

Michael's smile sent her stomach into chaos. The fish and chips had better be a while away.

She choked on her laughter. 'Might've been wiser than salmon fishing.'

He groaned. 'What happened?'

'I never learnt when to stay still, always went one step too far—and I fell in, filled my waders with freezing water straight from the mountains every time.'

'Did you catch any salmon?'

She shook her head. 'They were totally safe when I was around.'

'I tried trout fishing in Taupo once. I'd rather be running around a rugby field.'

'You miss it?' It must've been hard for him to give up when he was still a rising star.

'Yes and no. The body's too old to take the knocks now. I like to win—don't take coming second very well.'

That was what had lifted his game from good to exceptional, or so his coaches had said in one article she'd read online.

He drank down half his glass of beer. 'It wasn't easy, giving up a lifelong dream, especially when it seemed half the world was watching me.'

'It was your choice?'

'Yes, it was—and I don't regret it.'

He must be strong to do that. At a young age the temptation to stay in the limelight would've been hard to ignore. She needed to follow his example as she got on with living back here. Days like today would occur occasionally, but she couldn't let them decimate her. Her reaction to the birth of those twins had to be a one-off—anguish to be dealt with and put away. She needed to be strong, too.

A big, warm hand covered one of her smaller, chilled ones. 'Tell me?'

He could see her thoughts? Probably not hard when her mouth wasn't lifted in a smile any more, her hands had grown cold and her body had sagged forward.

'I had IVF once.'

He didn't look shocked, only sad for her. 'You lost your baby?'

'I didn't get that far. Thank goodness. It was

bad enough not conceiving with all the help available, but to get pregnant, feel your babies grow inside your belly and then lose them is beyond my comprehension.'

'But you came close to understanding today?'

Oh, God. This wasn't easy. Yet it felt good to tell Michael. She hadn't talked about this to anyone since Freddy had left her.

'I was probably way off the mark, but, yes, I hurt. For Melanie. For me. For those babies. Hers and the ones *I* can't have.'

Michael was up and around the table, sliding in beside her, his arm around her shoulder bringing her close to his warm body.

'You're resilient. You might've had a wee moment in ED, but then you straightened up and got on with your job—saving others.'

It hadn't been that easy, but she had found an inner strength. 'Thank you,' she whispered.

He pushed her glass towards her. 'Were you married or in a relationship?'

'Married for four years. Thought it was for ever. We both did. But the pressure of undergoing fertility treatment was hard…having it fail was much worse. We didn't survive.'

Gulping at the beer, she thought back to Freddy and his tears the day he'd told her he couldn't stay any longer, that he'd given all he had, his tank was empty.

'I don't blame Freddy for going. It was one

of those mazes neither of us could find a way out of.'

Counselling might have worked, if Freddy had agreed to attend, but he'd refused. He was a man, and men didn't *do* spilling their hearts to strangers. Not him, anyway. Not even for her, no matter how much she'd pleaded. Over was over, and he didn't want to be with her any more.

'He should've stuck to you like glue.' Michael was tense against her, his voice fierce. 'Not walked away when the going got tough.'

She pulled away from Michael's arm, slid along the seat to put space between them. Staying curled against him was making her punch-drunk. His defence of her was wonderful, but it undermined her determination to go it alone in her quest to get her future sorted and never be rejected by anyone again. She'd promised herself she'd get over Michael when she returned home—not fall in love with him.

'Freddy did the right thing for him, and ultimately for us. At first I hated him for going, but I've accepted the inevitability of it. If we couldn't survive that, we weren't as strong a couple as I believe couples should be.'

Their fish and chips arrived at that moment, and Stephanie didn't miss the relief pouring through Michael. He didn't have an answer to what she'd just said. Hell, she hadn't even known that was what *she* thought until thirty seconds ago. It was all new to her, but it felt absolutely right.

Tapping her glass against his, she smiled. 'Thanks for listening. I feel a lot better than I have at any time since picking up Melanie.'

Now she'd eat, and enjoy the fact that Michael had come out with her, before heading home to catch up on much needed sleep. Oh, and to tick another box—she'd found she might have the courage to stay put for ever this time.

She'd also told Michael about her infertility. So what? That wasn't on her list, no, but at least there'd be no ugly surprises in the future if they did spend more time together. Which they weren't going to do. Getting over him once and for all was the goal. The ultimate box to be ticked off.

But there was no denying he'd made her feel soft and warm when he'd got so uptight about Freddy. She didn't need anyone guarding her back, but that didn't mean it wasn't kind of cool when Michael did it.

CHAPTER THREE

'CARDIAC ARREST!' STEPH YELLED through to the front. 'I'm going to counter-shock.'

Waiting for Kath to pull over and stop, she checked the defibrillator that had been attached to their patient since they'd arrived at the factory where he worked as an electrician. She set it to start the moment Kath gave her the go-ahead.

'Go!' Kath called as she clambered through to join them.

'Stand back.' Steph punched the button on the machine.

Gavin Broad's body jerked, then slumped.

Kath watched the flat line on the defib screen. 'Negative.'

'Stand back.'

Another electric current whacked the man.

'We have a heartbeat. Erratic, but it's there.'

Kath continued to read the printout while Steph took his respiratory rate.

'Thank goodness for small miracles.'

Their man had mistakenly cut a live wire

with clippers that hadn't been insulated. His workmates had been quick to recognise that his heart had stopped and used the AED, but Gavin had arrested twice. A cardiologist was his best chance, and they weren't far from Auckland Central's ED.

Having to stop while applying the electric shock treatment was necessary for the patient's safety as well as Kath's and hers, but the delay sucked.

The ambulance lurched as Kath drove back out onto the road, sirens and lights going full blast. Steph focused on the heart monitor and on taking observations. This man was *not* going to die on her watch.

'Gavin, we're nearly at the hospital,' she told him. 'Then you'll be in expert hands.'

Michael's hands until the cardiologist arrived? He would pass up any case he was working on to take a stat one—unless another specialist was free already.

Her patient didn't react, just kept breathing shallowly. Not good, but at least he was alive. A third shock would be drastic, but she'd do it if she had to.

The ambulance swung in a wide circle, started backing up.

'We're here?'

'Yes, and we've got a reception committee waiting,' Kath answered.

She'd parked and had the back doors open as quickly as Steph had the defibrillator attached to the gurney and the Patient Report Form ready for handover.

'Who have we got?'

The question came from the man she'd been hoping to get a glimpse of.

'Gavin Broad, thirty-five, arrested twice.' Steph would've locked eyes with him, but he wasn't playing that game. However, he did take the PRF she held out. 'Initial failure due to a multiphase voltage event.'

With her at the head of the gurney and Kath at the other end they lowered it to the floor of the ambulance bay and rushed into the department. Urgency meant that the details would be gone through on the way.

'He's fortunate there was a defib on the premises.'

Michael strode beside the gurney. Even in ill-fitting scrubs there was no denying that magnificent body.

Not meant to be thinking like that.

Tell that to her hormones.

When he leaned towards their man to say, 'Hello, Gavin, I'm Dr Laing,' his broad shoulders filled her line of sight and stole the moisture from her mouth. They were wide, muscular, and she already knew how warm they could be.

Her hand tightened around the stretcher handle.

Don't forget he doesn't want a relationship with anybody.

Michael was talking to their patient as though Gavin was fully aware of everything. 'We're taking you into Resus, so we're prepared if another event happens. A cardiologist is on her way down to see you as I speak.'

Straightening up, those mouth-drying shoulders tight, he looked directly ahead as they rushed into Resus. No quick looks in her direction today.

Last night, after they'd got past her revelations and started on the fish and chips, they'd shared light-hearted banter. Aware that she wasn't getting over him in any way—more like getting more enamoured with him—she'd pulled the 'got to get some sleep' pin around eight-thirty and had ignored the slight widening of his eyes and tightening of his lips at the word 'sleep'.

Sleep...bed. There wouldn't be any sleep if they went to bed together. Not happening.

Today Michael was back to being the consummate professional, with no sideways glances in her direction, no acknowledging they'd had some down time together. *Grrr.* He was so good at that. What would rock him off balance?

Hello? How would that help with your need to get over him?

She had to try something, didn't she?

'Hear from Chantelle this morning?'

Michael looked down at the PRF in his hand. 'Nope, but nothing unusual in that.'

Unless Chantelle needed Michael to do something for Aaron.

Steph could read between the lines as well as anyone. She also knew when she was being ignored. There was a paramedic beside him—not the woman he'd shared an evening with. He was right. This wasn't the place for being disgruntled about his attitude. Except everyone around here usually took the time to be friendly, even if only with a sharp nod as they raced to save a patient.

In Resus, Steph took her place by Gavin and gripped the bedding, nodded to the other medical staff waiting. 'One, two, three.'

Gavin was instantly surrounded with ED staff and the cardiologist who'd walked in right behind them. Steph detached the ambulance defibrillator so the Resus unit could come into play.

Michael was talking to the cardiologist as a junior doctor listened to Gavin's heart through his stethoscope. Nurses were taking obs, attaching wires, monitors, and all the paraphernalia required to obtain the information to save Gavin if he went into arrest again.

She was no longer required. This wasn't her domain any more.

Walking away was easy. She might have loved working in here, been right at home with all the cases, the staff, the urgency, but she had all that and more now as a paramedic. Racing to a scene, lights flashing, sirens screaming, had her heart pounding and the adrenalin flowing. There were cases like Melanie's when she hated not having senior medical back-up, but those made her dig ever deeper to do all she could and more.

She began pushing the gurney out of Resus.

On Kath's belt the radio spewed a volley of words, their tone calm but urgent. 'Ambulance three, cyclist versus vehicle, intersection Grafton Road and Symonds Street.'

Kath answered. 'Roger, base. Grafton Road and Symonds Street. ETA five.'

As Steph picked up her pace she glanced over her shoulder. Michael was watching her, but immediately dropped his eyes when he knew she'd seen him.

Okay. Not sure what that meant, and don't have time to think about it. Shove the gurney in, click the wheel locks, slam the doors shut, buckle up and go.

Oh, yeah, this job rocked.

Kath spun the ambulance out of the dock, flicked on the warning gear. 'Head and shoulder injuries are cyclists' most likely damage. Then internal injuries.'

'Why do people get so passionate about bikes when they can get knocked off without trying?'

'Why do people cross roads on foot in peak traffic?' Kath braked as a car pulled out in front of them. 'Get out of the way, moron! What part of flashing lights and screeching siren don't you understand?'

With a glance in the rearview mirror and to the side, she jerked the heavy vehicle right into the oncoming lane which drivers had hurriedly vacated.

Steph laughed at this side of Kath, who was the picture of politeness when she was around patients. Needing to vent at people's total lack of concern for others in need of help was completely understandable.

'I could give them the finger,' she said. 'But I like my job too much.' Saying something out of anyone's hearing was one thing, making a public gesture would be going too far.

Kath chuckled, then sobered. 'Looks like that's our number—up ahead on the left-hand corner.'

As she parked Steph clambered through to the back to grab their equipment before dropping out through the back door and heading to the body sprawled on the road surrounded by people.

'Excuse me—stand back.'

One look and she knew this wasn't good.

On her knees, she said to the woman, 'Hi, I'm Steph—a paramedic.' She reached for a wrist, found an erratic pulse. 'What's your name?'

'Alison Knowles.'

Good response. 'Do you remember what happened?'

'Not really.' Her speech was bubbly and difficult to understand. but she continued talking. 'One minute I was cycling through the intersection…the next I was face-down on the road.'

Literally, if the swelling under her jaw and the missing front teeth were indicators. Alison had done quite the face-plant.

'I told the cops a van cut through a red light and collected her,' a man standing nearby informed them. 'Got her smack in the middle of his van and sent her flying through the air.'

'Better than going underneath the van,' someone else noted.

Kath had pads for the heart monitor attached to Alison's now exposed chest.

Steph stood up and looked around at the crowd. 'Thanks for helping this lady, folks, but can you now move back and give her some privacy while we attend to her?'

A uniformed cop pushed through. 'I'll take care of this.'

His shoulders were tight and his head high. He had a job to do. One he should've already been doing, but what had to be bum fluff on his jaw suggested he was hardly out of kindergarten, let alone the police academy.

Steph swallowed the impulse to grin. 'Thanks. The further back the better.'

Like the other side of the road.

Back on her knees, she asked her patient, 'Did you roll yourself over or did someone help you?'

'Two guys.' Her face was white and her eyes were glazing. 'I think…'

They should've left her as she was, in case there was damage to the neck and spinal cord.

'We're going to put a neck brace on. I need you to remain as still as possible while we do that, okay?'

Steph and Kath worked fast, asking questions, taking obs, checking Alison's head for trauma, then her shoulders, and finding the left clavicle was broken, and her right knee twisted, possibly dislocated.

Steph drew up some morphine. 'I'm going to give you some pain relief before we load you on the stretcher.' Not that it would negate all the pain, but any relief was better than none.

Alison didn't answer.

Kath shone a light in her eyes, got a small blink. 'Fading consciousness.'

Once the morphine had been administered they prepared to shift the woman onto the stretcher, with the help of two strong-looking bystanders. With Alison slipping in and out of consciousness time was important.

They were quickly loaded and the cop had the traffic stopped to let them out onto the road back towards Auckland Central.

'Impact injury to the right shoulder and hip,'

Steph reported with surprise, seeing Michael when they arrived back at the emergency department.

Why did *he* have to be the one she handed over to every time today? Doctors didn't usually rush to meet them unless it was a Code One job. Was he on the lookout for her when he heard the ambulance bay bell ring? But he'd been ignoring her earlier. *Men.* Who could understand them? Not her, for sure.

'Trauma to the skull?' he asked as he scanned the PRF she'd handed him.

'Soft area at the front of her cranium, injury to the jaw and cheekbones.'

Further tests, including X-rays, would be needed.

As Steph began pushing the stretcher into the department Michael took the other side. *Huh?* Had he forgotten he was the doctor, not the nurse or paramedic? Had he forgotten he wasn't talking to her?

He glanced across at her and said quietly, so no one else would hear, 'Is this why you changed careers? You're an adrenalin junkie and speeding around with flashing lights turns you on?'

There was a level of censure in his voice that grated.

'Yes, that's *exactly* why I'm a paramedic. We get loads of attention, racing through the streets,' she snapped.

What was *this* about? They'd got on well last night, with Michael being so understanding about her infertility.

'That explains it.'

Now he was smiling that gut-clenching, heart-speeding smile, as if he was on a mission to upset her and winning.

Drawing a calming breath, moderating her tone when she wanted to yell at him, she said, 'I haven't really changed. I still care for people who are hurting one way or another.'

They'd reached a resus room, and as everyone moved Alison across to the bed Steph gulped back unexpected tears. If he didn't want anything to do with her then he should just say so. He knew how to—had done it before.

Picking up the blanket, she turned to head back to the ambulance, leaving Kath to fill the medics in on their patient. She had a gurney to stow, equipment to tidy away, new blankets to place ready for their next call.

'Steph—wait.'

Michael appeared beside her.

'I'm all out of sorts today. Didn't get much sleep. But I shouldn't be taking it out on you when you're not the cause. I know how much you care about your patients. I really do.' His fingers shoved through his hair, displaced the errant curls on his forehead. 'Can we catch up tonight?'

'I don't think so.' Not very forgiving of her.

Okay. 'Can I answer that later, when I know if I have to pick my parents up from the airport or not?'

'No problem.'

He headed back to Alison, who was now surrounded by doctors.

Kath joined her at the ambulance. 'You want to check how Melanie and her babies are doing? Here's your opportunity. The radio's quiet.'

Throughout the night she'd woken often with the sound of Melanie's pain ringing in her skull—only somehow in her dream it had become her own anguish. Familiar torment that had laid dormant for a few years but seemed all too happy to rise up and knock her for six now.

'I'll be quick.'

Fear and exhaustion greeted her through the PICU window. She didn't hang around, understanding that it wasn't her place, but was grateful to see the babies were still in their incubators, with mum and dad hovering over them. There was a long way to go, but they'd made it this far. A positive start.

The next time she went into the ED with a patient Michael was nowhere to be seen. He'd probably knocked off a couple of hours ago. As she and Kath would when they got back to base.

Yet, futile as it was, she still scoped the department for a glimpse of scrubs-clad long legs and thick, unruly dark hair that her fingers itched to touch—and still came up disappointed when relief should have been loosening her tense muscles.

His comments about her being a paramedic still rankled, despite his genuine apology. Something must have caused him to say it in the first place. Was it *her* he was out of sorts with? Or was it himself he was having trouble with?

The way Chantelle had exploded onto the scene to snatch up her son had hurt him. She'd seen it in his tight mouth and sorry expression, in the need in his eyes. Need for what? A child of his own?

Her blood chilled. There was her escape route. There was nothing she could do if he wanted a family, so she had to get over him. And she wasn't going to do it by taking off for places unknown again. No more running away. Even if it felt as if her heart was breaking.

She continued her inner debate all the way back to base, and while she topped up the ambulance, went out to the car park and got into her cute red sports car. She sure loved this machine...

But what if family *wasn't* the cause of that need underneath all those other emotions that had skittered through Michael's eyes? Chantelle was family, and it seemed he looked out for her and Aaron big-time. More than necessary? More than Chantelle wanted?

Michael took responsibility seriously. She'd seen that in the department, even during those two weeks when she'd been having the time of her life he'd made sure she was comfortable about everything. She guessed she'd never really known him—and chances were she wasn't about to learn any more.

Which was good, wasn't it? Wasn't it her goal to get over him? But did all goals have to be met? Or could she change her mind? Go after him instead of trying to shove him back into a box labelled *Man Best Forgotten*?

A yawn sneaked up on her. There hadn't been a lot of sleep going on last night. Along with the rerun of negative pregnancy tests there'd been visions of Michael, lovingly holding his nephew. Pictures had rolled through her head on a circuit, waking her again and again.

Michael was committed to watching out for his sister and his nephew. He was committed to his work. He gave and gave—at home and in the department. Yet he said he didn't want commitment with anyone else. What did he do for himself? Did he have a secret hobby, like collecting stamps?

Steph laughed around another yawn. She could not picture that at all.

Waiting for the car's heater to do its thing before heading to the supermarket for something boring to eat, she felt an intense loneliness roll over and around her. It was like nothing she'd known before—not even when Freddy had left her in those bleak days when nothing had gone her way.

Now she was back in Auckland—seeing her parents regularly, getting to know her new work colleagues, and installed in her own home with all her possessions around her—she shouldn't feel despondent. This was what she wanted. *Wasn't it?*

How often had she said that? Starting out in Queenstown, then in London, in Italy... Her sigh was sour. Tonight was different. She wanted this and more. There was so much love in her heart, still waiting to be shared. What was wrong with her that she couldn't find a man to love her for who she was? A man who wouldn't reject her when the going got tough?

A text landed in her phone.

Don't need picking up. Got back on earlier flight and took taxi. Going to bed early, exhausted. Love Mum.

So, home or Michael's? Home was safe. Michael's was fraught with emotions she didn't want to face tonight.

Undecided, she put the car into 'drive' and

headed for the supermarket. Wherever she went she needed food. And maybe a bottle of wine.

Michael heard the low roar of a car in his driveway as he quietly closed Aaron's door. The kid had been fighting sleep for an hour but finally he'd succumbed. The last thing he needed was for him to wake again.

He knew who'd driven up. She hadn't phoned to tell him she'd be around, and yet he'd delayed phoning the Thai restaurant to put his order in.

Opening the front door, he leaned a shoulder against the frame. 'Your parents got home all right?'

Stephanie grinned up at him from the bottom step. 'All by themselves.'

He laughed. 'You wouldn't have taken that matchbox on wheels to collect them, would you?'

'Why not?' Her grin widened, then was stolen by a yawn. 'Sorry. Am I too late to add fried rice with pork to your order?'

She was standing in front of him now. He breathed her in. Honey and hot toast. Mouthwateringly delicious.

'Hello?' Stephanie waved a hand in front of him. 'Anyone home?'

'Don't know. I'll go find out.' He stood back to let her in, then remembered what she'd asked. 'I haven't ordered yet.'

'So you really *do* eat Thai on Tuesdays? Then this is perfect.' She handed him a bottle of Pinot Gris.

His heart slowed. 'You remembered.'

'Your favourite wine? Of course I did.'

There was no 'of course' about it. Two years was a long time to remember trivia.

Stephanie prefers Oomph-brewed coffee to Wake Up.

Okay, he got it.

She used to go crazy whenever I kissed a trail of kisses below her ear.

Michael slammed the door shut, wincing as he remembered the barely sleeping Aaron, and headed for the kitchen and some glasses. He needed a drink. Like right now. So much for trivia.

The kitchen was a mess, with plastic bowls and spoons and a fork littering the little table Aaron had used, with matching dollops of mashed pumpkin and potato on the floor.

'Tonight was an epic battle. But Aaron's finally, *finally* asleep. I hope.'

He shouldn't have said he was here. The questions were already lighting up in Stephanie's eyes.

'Chantelle was asked to work tonight. She fills shelves at the supermarket part-time.'

'Impressive.'

'She doesn't have to do it. I've offered to pay her university fees so she doesn't have to get a student loan or borrow for everyday expenses.' Stubborn didn't begin to describe his sister.

'She's got a child, is studying for a degree and works when you've given her an out? Even more impressive.' Stephanie twisted the cap off the bottle and took the glasses he'd lifted from the shelf.

'That's all very well, but she's constantly exhausted. And then there are the days I get Aaron because she's doing too much.'

'You don't *want* to look after him? I'm not believing that.'

He took the glass she offered. 'I adore my time with him. Watching him grow from a tiny baby to where he's at now, running and crashing, spitting out words in excitement over a moth crawling across the floor—I wouldn't miss that for anything.'

'So what's the problem? Seems to me Chantelle is doing a great job making a life for her son.'

He didn't like the way those lovely eyes were drilling into him, searching for answers to her questions. She wasn't getting them.

Snatching up the dishcloth, he bent to wipe up the mess. 'You're right,' he acknowledged, hoping that would shut her down.

'Want me to phone our order through?' she asked.

Relief loosened his tongue. 'The number's on speed dial on my phone. I'll have pork green curry—hot. Just tell them Dr Mike and they'll know where to come.'

'Dr Mike?'

'I was eating there one night when one of the cooks knocked a pan of boiling oil off the stove onto his leg. It was like a scene out of a horror movie, with oil everywhere, the guy screaming in agony, and blood from where his head hit the edge of the stove as he went down.'

'Is the cook all right now?'

'Good as new—if you don't count the scars.'

'Do they still charge you for meals?'

Her smile went straight to his heart. He cursed silently.

'They tried that one. Eat all I want as often as I want, for free.' He shook his head. 'I told them I'd go somewhere else if they didn't take payment, but now I get wontons or deep fried shrimps with every order.'

'Win-win. I like that.'

Her lips touched the rim of her glass and he watched as she took in a mouthful of wine.

That mouth, hot and slick on his skin, had been sensational, and it was another piece of trivia from two years ago. How had he found the strength to stop their affair? Must've needed his head read. Because right now he would not be able to stop if they were to start again.

'Here.' He thrust his phone at her. 'Order dinner.'

Her head tilted to one side. 'Yes, sir.' And she did as he'd demanded.

He'd been that close to reaching for her, removing the glass from her slim fingers and hauling her curvaceous body he'd been hankering after for two long days and nights up against him. He still was that close. Closer, because he'd taken a step nearer.

He needed to step back, because no way did he want to hurt Stephanie further down the track when he inevitably messed up.

But one kiss…?

'Bugsy's gone.'

Michael spun around to gape at his nephew, standing in the kitchen doorway rubbing his eyes. 'Hey, buddy, you're meant to be in bed.'

The little guy did have his uses. Stopping that potential hug, kiss, whatever might have followed, was mammoth.

'Bugsy. I want my monkey.'

'I'll find him.' Michael swept the little boy up into his arms, kissed his forehead. 'Bet he's hiding under the bed. That's his favourite place, isn't it?'

'Water!' Aaron cried.

'Of course.' Michael smiled.

Of course. And then it would be *I want a 'nana.*

'Stalling tactics?' Stephanie asked.

'You're on to it.' With one hand he filled a bottle with water from the fridge. 'There you go. Let's find Bugsy.'

'I want a 'nana.'

'You've had dinner.'

Aaron's mouth opened, the indignant cry already in his expression.

'All right—half a banana it is.'

'Softy,' Steph called from behind him.

'It's my middle name.'

Michael forked up rice and curry, chewed, swallowed. 'Tell me more about why you joined the ambulance service.'

Stephanie's fork banged onto her plate. 'We've already done this.'

'The flashing lights and screaming sirens bit, yes. But not the *real* reason that had you changing from a career you loved and were exceptional at.'

'Nothing like going from rugby to medicine?'

'Low blow.'

Tell her, it's no secret.

'My rugby career was stellar, yes, and at first I couldn't see past the hype and the excitement, the sheer thrill of playing in front of those large crowds. Two episodes of concussion wised me up, made me grow up. A third knock and doing anything as intense as becoming a doctor would've been in jeopardy. I'd always known rugby wasn't a lifelong career.'

'Not all players see it so clearly.'

'Unfortunately. But I do understand the attraction. It's exhilarating, being on the field with forty thousand people watching your team, cheering or booing—didn't matter, they were there because of us.'

Stephanie pushed her near empty plate across the counter to the sink. 'In Queenstown I did a couple of stints on a rescue helicopter when they were short-staffed.' She sipped her wine. 'I got a taste for the adventure—the thrill and the scary stuff. And then, while I was in London, an opportunity came up to do three months on the ambulances and I figured I might as well give it a go.'

When the silence spread out too long he coaxed her. 'There's more to it, Steph.'

Her eyes widened. 'Caught!' Her forefinger drew circles on the countertop. 'When I decided to return home I didn't want to slip back into the same groove I was in before I left. I didn't want to find that after a few months the two years I'd been away were smothered and that despite my experiences away from Auckland nothing had changed. *I* hadn't changed.'

That made sense. But what was behind it all? Infertility and a broken marriage would do it.

And it had him on the back foot, afraid of hurting her again. Everyone he was close to he hurt eventually. Stephanie had had enough to contend with. It was time for her to have fun and laughter and love—things he couldn't trust himself to deliver.

During those two intense weeks they'd had together he'd have sworn she was well on the road to recovery. And yet that dreadful sadness knocking her off her toes yesterday showed she still ached over the past.

'So you're home for good?' He didn't know why, but he needed to know.

She nodded emphatically. 'Definitely. I loved travelling, and working in different places, but I'm a home body. This is where I know myself.'

His eyes drank in the sight of that body as she sat on a high stool opposite him, her elbows on the counter, her hands holding her glass. Curves, hand-sized breasts, that pert bottom… His groin tightened as her tongue licked her lips. It hadn't been getting much exercise for a long time.

Honey teased his senses again. Was it her shampoo? What else could it be?

Honey was one of his favourite things—liquid gold on hot toast and melted butter. His mother's treat when he was little.

His upper body leaned in so Stephanie was close enough for him to feel her heat. *Honey.* His mouth watered. Then dried as her tongue repeated that licking thing. Did she know she was doing that? How the hell was he supposed to turn away when his groin was thick with need?

His hand was on her upper arm, tugging her gently closer, so her body was lined up against his. His other hand raised her chin so he could dive into those enormous toffee-coloured eyes.

'Stephanie…' he whispered, and stood up, bringing her with him.

Her body tightened and she waited, holding her breath. Then, 'Michael…'

And she sank into him, her sweet mouth accepting his, opening for his exploring tongue. Giving him a kiss like those she'd given him two years ago. Hot, demanding, giving. All Steph.

'Stephanie.'

The air closed in around them, held them in a bubble. The world had reduced to just them. How long they stood there, their bodies locked together, their kiss endless, he did not know. He could have stayed for ever—until kisses weren't enough.

His hand found hers, grasped it to pull her along to his bedroom. 'Come with me.'

He was all but begging. Would beg if he had to.

Her fingers laced through his. 'Michael…'

She stopped. Then doubt entered her eyes, slapped him upside his head.

'I've got to go.'

*Really? When your body is as awakened as
mine? When we want each other?*

'Okay.'

That was all he said as he unclasped his hand
with difficulty, not about to force himself on her.
She either wanted to go to bed with him or she
didn't, and he wasn't hanging around for her to
change her mind.

'Okay.'

Sometime tomorrow, or next month, he might
be glad she'd pulled the plug, but right at this moment he could almost be angry about it. *Almost.*
Because she was probably the sane one around
here at the moment.

CHAPTER FOUR

STEPH WOUND THE music up full blast in an attempt to drown out her brain and its ranting.

Stupid...crazy. Why kiss the man? Didn't she know how that would make her feel? How she'd keep wanting more?

She had the left side of her brain to thank for her not going to bed with him. If she'd listened to the right side instead she'd now be having an amazing time in bed with the sexiest man on the planet.

The left front wheel bumped on the kerb as she pulled into her drive. Braking hard, she snapped the ignition off. Why had she gone to Michael's in the first place? All very well thinking she had to get over him, but she'd only succeeded in making things worse.

She still wanted him. After years of having nothing to do with him her hormones craved his body, his smile, those kisses. She wanted him and cared about him more than ever.

Absence makes the heart grow fonder.

Yeah, right—and it also mucked up a girl's thinking.

Folding her arms on the steering wheel, she banged her useless head down on her forearms. Now what? Michael would have recognised her reaction for what it was—*need*. For *him*. Hopefully he hadn't seen her real feelings…

He started it.

Truly? The fact that she'd plastered herself to his body and willingly kissed him didn't make it seem as if she'd been fighting him off.

Where should she move to next? Wellington? Australia? Her heart sagged.

No, please no more moving around looking for the impossible.

The impossible was right here on her doorstep in the form of one sexy, beautiful, wonderful man. Returning home had always been full of difficulties, and this was just one of them.

Just? When her heart was still thumping and her core ached for him?

She should have taken what was on offer. If she couldn't assign Michael to the 'has been loved' bucket maybe she should make the most of any opportunity to have fun with the man.

Her phone interrupted that stupid thought.

Michael. He clearly hadn't ditched her number when he'd ditched her.

Don't answer.

'Hello?'

'You get home all right?'

'Yes.'

'Good. See you tomorrow.'

He wouldn't. She had two days off. 'Bye.'

Auckland sure was testing her. Making sure she really intended putting her feet on the ground permanently and not running away again. Well, she was going to pass these tests with flying colours, even if her heart got dented along the way. She had to. The alternative wasn't worth considering. She was done with being lonely. And if she got hurt on the path to finding happiness she'd deal with it. *Here.*

Eight-oh-five. A veritable sleep-in. Stumbling into the kitchen, Stephanie turned up the heat pump before filling the kettle. It took a cup of tea to wake up properly. Pouring muesli into a bowl, she found her thoughts straight away turning to Michael and how to act next time she saw him. Thankfully she wasn't on days again until Friday. He'd have forgotten he'd kissed her by then.

But if that kiss had affected him half as much as it had her it would hang between them like a tolling bell. *Bang, bang, bang.* Great kiss. Bad reaction. Could they do it again?

She only had herself to blame for her uptight state. She could have walked away before they got started. She hadn't. End of story. Get over it.

People kissed all the time. Didn't mean the world had come to an end. Not even hers.

A low whine came from outside. A dog?

Pushing the curtains wide, she blinked at the sight of the black and tan dog shivering up against the sliding glass doors.

'Who are you, lovely?' Opening the slider, she gasped at the cold, wet air enveloping her. 'It's freezing out here.'

Rubbing her hand over soft, damp fur got her a gentle head-nudge before the most adorable pleading eyes focused on her.

'You're beautiful, aren't you?'

Thump, thump. Its tail whacked the wooden deck.

She glanced under its belly. 'Well, boy, I don't know what you're doing here, but this isn't your house.' There were tags on his collar. Council registration and a name. 'Zac.'

Thump, thump.

A wind gust drove rain under the overhang, straight at her. And Zac. Straightening up, she stepped backwards through the door and the dog followed.

'Hey, I don't think you should come in. You don't belong here.'

But pushing him outside wasn't really an option when he was still shivering and now she'd seen how his ribs pushed at his skin and the concave shape of his belly.

'I don't have any dog food…'

There was plenty of meat in the freezer, put there by her dad for when the family dropped by for a barbecue—which hadn't happened yet, because someone always seemed to be out of town at the moment. When they finally all caught up at the same time for one of those family dos she might start feeling more at home in her house. At the moment it was empty and cold, as though the rooms were waiting for people, laughter, lots of talking. Things her family would provide in shovelfuls.

Setting the microwave on defrost, Steph placed a pack of steak inside and then dried Zac off with an old towel. Next she filled a bowl her mother had given her for a birthday with water, and sighed happily as the dog lapped the liquid up. Her visitor was cute and he gave her the warm fuzzies.

While Zac gulped the meat down she poured another mug of tea. 'I'm going out soon. The dentist's beckoning.' *Shudder.* 'You'll have to go home then.'

The dog dropped to the floor, laid his head on his paws and stared up at her with that pleading look back in his eyes.

'You can't stay here. Someone must be missing you.'

He was heart-meltingly beautiful. And her heart was responding to that plea. Too much.

Someone out there must be frantic, wondering where he was.

Four hours later, when she returned from retail therapy, trying to dissipate the discomfort produced by a heavy-handed dental technician cleaning her teeth, Zac was still there, leaning against the door she'd found him at earlier. He bounded up, his tail wagging as he nudged her butt with his head.

'You're a naughty boy. You were meant to go home. I'm not getting any more meat out of the freezer.'

She sighed. Or maybe she was.

'I'll ring the council dog pound and find out if anyone's been asking for you.'

What if they hadn't? Could she keep him? *Melt, melt*, went her heart. It wouldn't be fair. She worked twelve-hour shifts four days in a row. What would she do with him on those days? It didn't matter. Zac might look a little malnourished, but his coat gleamed now she'd dried it and he hadn't cowered from her once. He was well looked after. Someone out there was missing him.

'Zac belongs to a Mrs Anderson. She hasn't been in touch to report him missing so she might be away. We'll be investigating. She should've made arrangements for the dog if that's the case.'

The woman at the pound ranted on for inter-

minable minutes when Steph rang the council.
She also gave her over Mrs Anderson's address.

Should the woman be telling her those details?

'Will you phone and tell her I can drop Zac
off?' Steph asked. She was more than happy to
deliver her new friend home, since he came from
a street only a couple of blocks away.

'The ranger will be round pick up the dog later
this afternoon.' *Click.*

Fine. Thanks. Why give her the address, then?
'Someone's going to take you home.' She rubbed
the silky head resting on her thigh. 'Isn't that
great?'

There went any idea of keeping him.

There were a few text messages on her phone
she hadn't heard coming in. One from Michael.

Kelli's dropping in to the department around
two if you want to catch up.

Kelli and her fake engagement to Mac, which
became real. A true love-match—even if it *had*
taken some teasing to bring it out into the open.

The last time she'd seen those two had been
at her farewell drinks in the bar over the road
from Auckland Central Hospital, before she'd
moved to Queenstown. All loved-up and happy
beyond description.

Will do.

Having texted him back, she knew there was no avoiding Michael now. His message hadn't given her any clues as to what he was thinking about her, though if he'd wanted to avoid her he wouldn't have sent it in the first place. He could have denied still having her number. Why *did* he still have it?

Woof.

'You, my boy, are going outside again.'

She wouldn't be here when the ranger arrived to pick him up, but there was nothing she could do about that. Probably for the best anyway. It would take very little to tempt her into keeping him.

'Steph, look at you! You haven't changed a bit.'

Kelli's arms wrapped around her the moment they saw each other. Hugging her back, Steph laughed. 'Still exaggerating everything.'

'I wouldn't.' Kelli pulled back and glanced around before saying, 'Michael's as good-looking as ever—and still single, I hear.'

'Apparently so.' How did she stop heat pouring into her cheeks? 'What've you and Mac been up to since I last saw you?'

'You and I need to catch up for lunch one day when you're not working.' Kelli grinned. 'As for us—making babies.'

'You're pregnant again?'

For once the usual hollowed-out sensation didn't hit her with its full debilitating hardness, but her stomach still dropped to her knees and her heart landed in her throat. Babies—babies everywhere. Just not for her. It still sucked, big-time, but she wouldn't let that show—couldn't dull Kelli's happiness because of these selfish feelings.

Throwing her arms back around Kelli, the nurse she'd worked alongside when she was going through her own version of hell, she said, 'That's the best news I've heard in a long time.'

It truly is, so get out of my throat and back behind my ribs, dear heart.

'I have to say your life's been dull if that's what it takes to cheer you up.'

'I don't need cheering up.' *Did she?* No, not at all.

'Hi, there, Stephanie—glad you got my text.'

The man with the deep and husky voice stood behind her.

Turning slowly, to give herself time to fix her features into neutral, she faced Michael. 'Thanks for the text. I'd have hated to miss Kelli.'

'No problem. Why aren't you working? Some-thing wrong?'

She cleared that concern out of his eyes with, 'I'm on days off. I did four day shifts this round, but next I'm up for days and nights.' She wasn't ill, or sulking because of last night, if that was what he was thinking.

'Six-day weeks? You don't mind?'

She shrugged. 'Comes with the territory.'

Later on, if she got involved with someone or took up playing netball again, she might be irked at having to work weekends, but at the moment it made no difference.

There was a gentle poke at the back of her waist. 'Don't go without giving me your phone number,' murmured Kelli, before crossing to talk to someone else she knew.

Don't leave me alone with Michael. I'm not sure what to say to him.

But Steph couldn't help glancing at him, and instantly looked away from the dynamic gaze that seemed stuck on her. 'What?'

'Nothing.'

'Good.'

'Chantelle arrived minutes after you left.'

So if she'd gone down the hall last night, instead of walking out through the front door, who knew what his sister would have discovered?

'You must be glad I'd left.'

Her heart dropped. It was beginning to make sense. His life was devoted to work and to his extended family, with no room for anyone else other than grabbed moments over a meal or in bed. No room for her other than he needed to scratch an itch.

Was she his itch?

'She wasn't meant to be picking Aaron up until the morning. But, considering I'm never one hundred percent certain she'll do what she says, I should've been more circumspect.'

Deflate me, why not?

'Seems late for Aaron to be going home.'

She shouldn't have said that. It sounded judgemental. It *was* judgemental.

'Sorry—none of my business.'

His sister must drive him bonkers at times. Though he was far more patient than she'd ever be.

'Now you know how it is in my house.'

Don't you mean in your life? But, yeah, buster, the picture's getting clearer by the minute.

If he thought he had to warn her to stay away he had nothing to worry about. After last night she had no intention of ever dropping by again. A girl could only be so stupid before she wised up.

'I'd better go after Kelli.'

'See you around.'

Her heart sank. Back to square one. He could kiss her senseless and wave her off without a hint of reluctance in that sexy voice. More fool her for letting it get to her.

Sit up, heart, and start clapping as if you're

grateful he's like this. We don't want him back in our life.

Kelli nudged her gently. 'Smile like you're happy. At the moment he's going to think you're upset with him.'

I am.

Stretching her lips she asked, 'Better?'

'Looks like you've got a mouthful of vinegar. Now, what's your number?'

While pretending to read a patient's notes Michael watched Steph talking with Kelli as though she didn't give a toss that he was here—ten metres away. As if kissing him senseless had been just *ho-hum.*

He'd have sworn she'd been as ready for him as he had her last night. That supple body had moulded to his and she'd all but had to peel herself off him when she'd chosen to leave.

Even Chantelle barrelling in to collect Aaron hadn't cooled his ardour. At night once Aaron was asleep there was no waking him—which was why he hadn't thought anything of heading to the bedroom with Stephanie.

He was hugely grateful not to have been caught with Stephanie, but there was nothing else that made him happy about her walking out.

Chantelle would have had plenty to say about where his obligations lay. And that would be with her and Aaron, and Carly if needed, not with an outsider.

Chantelle had once nearly cost him his job in another ED when she'd needed too much of his time and concentration. There wasn't room for a meaningful other half in his life and risk it all crashing and burning around his feet again. So, yes, he'd dodged another bullet. So had Stephanie.

Across the room, she and Kellie were bent double with laughter, shaking their heads at each other. Steph, when she laughed, was another woman. Soft and cute and so lovely. She was all those things most the time.

Last night he'd wanted to haul her down to his bedroom and press her to the sheets, make love to her until she begged him to stop. Then and only then would he have sunk into her heat and lost his mind. He owed her big-time for having the strength to leave, because in the end he wasn't available for more than those snatched moments and Stephanie deserved far more. She deserved permanence. Commitment. *Love.*

Michael froze. *Love?* Not from him. He'd screwed up one marriage by apparently not devoting enough time to his ex, and he couldn't promise Stephanie any more because of all his other commitments. A second failed marriage was *not* happening.

His gaze fixed on the woman playing with

his mind. She looked marvellous in those tight-fitting jeans and a thick woollen jersey that accentuated her breasts. Breasts he hadn't had the chance to hold, to kiss and lick and enjoy last night. Under his scrubs his groin tightened. This was lust—not love.

The squeaky, tight pulling in his veins, the out-of-rhythm beat of his heart—all of it was to do with the lust hardening below his belt. Nothing to do with love. He knew what love felt like—knew the agony and the ecstasy, the hollowed out sensation when it was withdrawn.

His marriage had lasted fifteen months, had ended in fireworks and national headlines, and proved he had the family 'no good at long-term' gene. Proved that he was not good at commitment.

His mum and dad had divorced when he was seven—his dad again six years later, after increasing his family by two. One half-sister had a divorce behind her, and the other refused to marry her partner. With that pedigree he wasn't prepared to take another gamble.

Yet Stephanie had stirred him up something terrible. Once again.

Stephanie. His blood was always warmer when she was around. Hotter, thicker.

She was still with Kelli, her head tipped back as she listened, that thick hair shaped around her slim neck so tempting his fingers itched.

She hadn't been laughing when Kelli had said she was pregnant. There'd been a sharp stab of pain in the back of her eyes. Quick to show, quicker to disappear, but now he knew to look for it it had been obvious.

Yes, taking her to bed was high on his list of needs. But it wasn't going to happen.

Anything else he wanted also had to be ignored.

And if that made him cruel then he'd put his hand up. He could not stop wanting her, because it was the wrong thing to do, but he could and would keep her at arm's length.

He picked up the phone and punched in the number for PICU. Stephanie would want an update on those twins.

So much for arm's length.

'This is Con from the dog pound. I'm at your address now and there's no sign of the dog you called in.'

Steph's heart sank as she pulled off the road and held her phone hard against her ear. 'I couldn't find anything safe to tie him up with.'

'I've been around to where he lived with Mrs Anderson and he's not there either. The neighbours say they haven't seen him since the day she was found dead.'

'What do you mean?'

Con sighed. 'Three days ago concerned neighbours broke into her house and found her deceased in bed.'

'That's awful.'

For everyone. No wonder Zac was wandering the streets. He was hungry and lonely and desperate.

'Does anyone want him? Family? A friend or neighbour?' She held her breath.

'Not that we've been able to ascertain. He'll most likely go up for adoption—if we can find him before it's too late.'

The man didn't have to say what that meant. She had a vivid imagination. 'I'll go for a walk—call out to him when I get home.'

She didn't have to.

'You're a persistent little guy, aren't you?'

Steph bent down to pat Zac, who'd raced to her car the moment she'd pulled into the drive. 'I have to let the ranger know you're here so he can pick you up.'

Didn't she?

Zac's head tipped to one side. He sensed that she was weakening?

Could she keep him? Adopt him?

Getting a pet would be another step in making her move home feel permanent. No way could she take off and leave him behind, and she couldn't take him overseas.

Hey, you're not going anywhere. This is home. Warts and all.

Dog and all?

'Zac, do you want to come live with me?'

'He's a German Shepherd Collie cross, with probably some other bits thrown in,' Con told her when she phoned him back. 'Two years old, fully vaccinated, no record of wandering until now.'

'Can I keep him?'

'I talked to your neighbour earlier and there's no problem with you taking him.'

That made her uncomfortable. She didn't know her neighbours very well. 'What do I have to do?'

'There's paperwork to fill in. We need a record of where he's gone in case anyone asks later on. But as of now he's yours.'

'Zac…'

Steph blinked and smudged tears away from her cheeks. How easy was that? She'd wanted someone to love. So the object of that love had four legs and a collar? Worked for her. Another box ticked.

Dropping to her knees, Steph wrapped her arms around her new housemate and sniffed hard. 'Welcome to my world, beautiful.'

She'd done it. This was a permanent step and there was no going back. Instantly exciting and frightening.

Her new life really was underway. She was now a paramedic with a dog, living in her own house. And she was facing up to Michael.

'Let's go shopping for doggie things.'

An hour later she drove through the streets towards home, Zac sat beside her, his head out of the window, catching the breeze. Her fingers tapped in time to the country song blasting out from the stereo and her mouth kept lifting into unbidden smiles.

Yeah, she'd done the right thing—for her *and* for Zac.

CHAPTER FIVE

'THIRTY-ONE-YEAR-OLD MALE, burns to left leg and foot caused by hydrochloric acid splashing when a glass cylinder fell and smashed,' Steph told the nurse meeting them in the ambulance bay at Auckland Central's ED. 'Matthew Brown, science teacher at Point Chev High.'

There'd been a lot of unnecessary panic going down in the classroom when she and Kath had arrived, which had taken longer to deal with than making their patient comfortable.

Kath handed over the PRF before helping Matthew on to the bed. Another case delivered into the care of experts.

Steph relaxed and looked around the department. Of course Michael wasn't here. It was Saturday and his weekend off. Disappointment hit her hard. He shouldn't affect her like this, but she looked for him every time they delivered a patient. Every single time.

'I'm going to grab a coffee to go,' Kath told

her once the stretcher was locked back in place inside their vehicle. 'Want one?'

'I'd kill for one. Fingers crossed we don't get called for the next five minutes.'

'I'll get them if you want to go see how those babies are doing.'

Did she? Last she'd heard the twins were improving as much as anyone could hope for, which Michael told her had to be the best news.

'Won't be long.'

Racing to the elevator, she went up to the neonatal unit only to be told that Melanie and the babies had been transferred to Auckland Women's.

'The babies are doing okay?' Was it a bad thing that they'd been sent across the city?

'They're doing fine,' said Sarah, the PICU nurse Steph gone to nursing school with. 'The specialist wanted them close to him so he can be on tap if anything changes.'

Which it could with such premature babies. 'That's good.'

Steph headed back to the ambulance and her coffee, her heart a little lighter for Melanie.

'One latte.' Kath handed her a paper cup with a grunt. 'It's turning into a long day.'

'Busy's good.' It left no time for sitting around thinking about the impossible—how to put Michael out of her head.

Kath blew on her long black. 'What have you got planned for tonight? A party or a hot date?'

If only.

Steph started up the ambulance and headed for base. 'Try a quiet night in with the dog.'

Kath spluttered into her coffee. 'You're kidding me, right?'

'Auckland Central Ambulance Three.' The dispatcher's voice came through loud and clear.

'Here we go again.' Saved by the radio.

Steph reached for the handpiece, but Kath beat her.

'Ambulance Three.'

Steph listened in as she negotiated the ambulance towards Karangahape Road, ready to turn at the lights in whichever direction they were needed.

'Thirty-six-year-old male, leg wound from tomahawk axe, severe bleeding. One-zero-five Albany Street, Parnell.'

One hundred and five Albany Street? Steph's heart hit her toes. *No way.* What would Michael be doing with a tomahawk? It would have to be very sharp to do severe damage. Air stuck in her lungs. If not Michael, then who?

'Roger, coms,' Kath responded, then repeated the address and details.

Struggling to find her calm mode, Steph concentrated doubly hard on traffic and loose cannon drivers who liked to beat a racing ambulance to the corner.

The siren seemed to screech louder than usual as she headed to Parnell. To Michael.

A shudder ripped through her. It might not be Michael. But she couldn't shake the feeling that it was.

'How do you chop your leg with a tomahawk?'

'Chopping kindling? But being distracted enough to hit your leg is beyond me.'

'I wonder who called it in?' Michael himself? Most likely.

'You know who lives at the address?' Kath asked.

'Michael Laing from the ED.'

'Ah…'

Steph didn't like the way that sounded. '"Ah", nothing. I was thinking that he's not going to be happy about being taken into his own department by us.'

She tapped the address into the GPS to see if there was a shorter route, as she only knew one way there.

'Or he might be so thrilled so see us he'll shout us a night out at Scarpio's. It's the best restaurant in town at the moment.'

Steph couldn't find a laugh. Not even a single chuckle.

'Get out of the way!' she snarled at the driver of a pickup truck blocking the intersection ahead. Her temper was not improved when the guy waved as they roared past.

This trip was taking for ever, and every kilometre gained seemed long and tortuous. Finally
Steph swung into Michael's drive and turned
off the siren. Kath was already in the back with
the kit in her hand, so Steph leapt out and ran.
Up the path, around the house and aimed for the
back porch, where Michael sat on the step, pale,
obviously in pain—and angry.

'Michael, what happened?'

She raced up the steps and dropped to her
haunches beside him, already reaching for the
blood-soaked jersey wound around his thigh,
with the fingers of his right hand splayed over
it, applying pressure to slow the bleeding. He
was shivering, shock clearly coming into play.

'Slow down. It's not an emergency. No need
for the siren either. Now the nosey neighbours
will be turning up to gawp.'

Nice to see you too. 'What happened?' she repeated. 'I need to know.'

'The neighbour's cat was fighting a stray and
chased it through here—right across my feet. I
didn't hear the hissing and snarling until it was
too late. I had only just finished sharpening the
blade this morning. I was distracted. And when
I knocked into the shed wall…'

Snapping on gloves, Steph began gently feeling for deep trauma in his thigh. It was a bad lac-
eration that possibly went through to the bone.
'When you do something you do it thoroughly.' It

must be extremely painful, though he was being stoic beyond belief.

A sudden indrawn breath had her looking up. Got that wrong. She caught him, putting her hands on his chest to stop him tipping sideways onto the porch.

'Easy does it.' Gripping his shoulders, she studied him as he opened his eyes slowly. He was obviously in agony. 'Deep breaths.'

He focused on her as his chest lifted.

'Breath out now.'

His chest stopped, held, then sagged.

Good. 'We'll get you on the stretcher.'

'Right here,' said Kath from behind her.

'I don't need that. I can walk to the ambulance.'

He started struggling to his feet, and there was a lot more swaying going on.

'Sit down,' Stephanie snapped.

She could do cranky too. Especially since Michael was hurt and not letting her help him.

'Now.'

To emphasis her point she pulled at his elbow until he obliged by sagging onto the step with little control.

'Be careful.'

This was a very different Michael from the one she knew.

He glared at her. '*I'm* the doctor here. We'll do it *my* way.'

Resisting the urge to run the back of her finger down his pale cheek and reassure him that she'd do everything he needed, she dug deep for a retort.

'I'm the paramedic, and in case you've forgotten that means *I'm* in charge at an accident scene.'

She couldn't have him thinking she was going soft on him.

'That jersey isn't doing a good enough job, so I'll have to remove it and wrap bandages around the wound.'

'Need some readings done too.' Kath added her bit as she reached for his left wrist and got growled at for her trouble.

'What's wrong with your wrist?' Steph asked.

He held it awkwardly. 'Must've cracked it when I fell over.'

Cracked or broken? 'When were you going to mention that?' she snapped, her patience wearing thin. 'Michael, we need to know *everything*. You understand that.'

The eyes looking at her were darker than she'd ever seen them before, filled with pain and anger—and a message she couldn't interpret. As if he was angry with her for some reason.

She was doing her job—nothing more or less. But her heart was thumping and her breathing was too fast.

Slowly drawing in a lungful of cold air, she

laid a hand on his shoulder and squeezed lightly. 'We won't make a big deal of anything, I promise.'

Finally he dragged his gaze away. 'Go ahead. I do know what you've got to do.' The sharpness had gone, and his voice was suddenly heavy and lethargic.

Until Kath said, 'Right, let's get you on the stretcher.'

'I'll make my own way, thank you very much.' But the curse he bit out afterwards wasn't that quiet.

'Michael, stop being an idiot. That injury is serious—as in probably needing surgery serious.'

'I know that,' he snapped.

He might be a doctor and know what was ahead, but he was also a man in pain, and clearly not looking forward to the coming hours.

'At the moment you're a patient.'

'It *has* dawned on me,' he snapped.

He wanted to walk to the ambulance so she'd give him that—but nothing more. If she slipped her arm around his waist what would he say?

She was about to find out. Swinging the kit over one shoulder, she put her arm around him, took a step, and stopped when he didn't join her.

'Stop hovering,' Michael growled.

He hated it that Stephanie was intent on hanging around right beside him—*with* him, *holding* him—ready to catch him if his head did that spinning, floating, not getting a grip on reality thing again.

As if *she* could hold him off the ground. She was small and soft—he was big and muscular. Didn't she realise that he could do her some damage? He should've taken the offer of the stretcher. Was he going soft in his old age? He'd taken plenty of hard knocks playing rugby and not once been stretchered off. Nothing was changing today. He might be acting like a prat, but a man was entitled to his pride.

'Where are your house keys?' Steph asked in her professional voice.

He'd hurt her with his determination not to let her help him, but that was who he was—how he'd got through the painful take-downs on the rugby field, how he'd survived a broken heart.

He groaned in pain and frustration. Why Stephanie and Kath, when there were dozens of ambulance crews working in the city? What were the odds? It seemed that when it came to Stephanie and him they were fairly short.

'Hello? I asked a question. As a patient you're supposed to answer so I know how alert you are.'

Was that a hint of a smile lifting the left corner of her mouth? Doubtful. He didn't deserve one.

'They're on the kitchen bench.'

'I'll get them once you're loaded.' She shook her head. 'Obviously you shouldn't be left in charge of an axe. Getting distracted is plain dumb.'

'Do you talk to all your patients like this?'

He knew she didn't but she needed redirecting. Otherwise next he'd be spilling the reason why he'd been 'plain dumb'. That would go down a treat. She'd probably leave him on the pavement and hurl that ambulance down the road, siren screaming, putting as much space between them as possible.

Because he would've seen and heard that blasted cat a lot earlier if Stephanie hadn't been prowling around inside his skull.

'Only the difficult ones.'

Her words slapped at him hard, unlike her light and yet assured fingers when she'd checked out his leg.

Kath had the gurney locked back in place inside the ambulance and was reaching for his arm.

'This is going to hurt.'

At least she didn't sound pleased about it, whereas Stephanie was probably shrieking with laughter on the inside.

A small but surprisingly strong hand took his other arm.

'Let's do it.'

Her fingers squeezed encouragement.

A quick glance at Stephanie's face told him

she didn't want him hurting at all. Why was he being so stubborn? Because he didn't want her to think he needed her help? He'd hurt her once by walking away before they got too involved— he wasn't about to let her close again. She'd had her share of sorrows, and she didn't need him adding any more. Because in the end he would. It was in his genes.

Biting down hard he took his first step, followed it up with a second, then a fast stumble to get inside the ambulance, groping with his good hand for the stretcher to collapse on to and take the pressure off.

The names he was silently calling himself for being so stubborn were unprintable. To put it bluntly, Stephanie was right: he was an idiot, a really stupid, dumb idiot…

'Mike? What the—?'

His head flipped up. 'Jock? Sorry, I got a bit tied up and forgot to phone you. I can't make it tonight.'

They were supposed to be going for a beer before heading to Eden Park for the rugby game of the year between the Auckland and Wellington provincial teams. A game he'd been hanging out for ever since the beginning of the season.

'Kind of reached that conclusion myself. What have you done now?'

'Seems he's not the macho forestry man with an axe he thought he was.' Stephanie pushed around his friend and climbed into the ambulance.

'He what?' Jock stared at Stephanie for a long moment, then fixed that annoying, oh, so sharp look back on him. 'You copped an *axe*?'

'Something like that.' Michael stared straight back. It was easier than watching Stephanie work on his leg.

Jock saw through him and grinned, but he wasn't hiding the concern in his face. 'Glad you're not a surgeon, mate.'

Michael chose to ignore that concern, given how his friend was probably already thinking up ways to make a joke at his expense. 'Make yourself useful and lock up the house for me, will you?'

'Will do—and then I'll follow you to the ED. Someone's got to keep an eye on you.'

Jock turned to Stephanie and Kath. 'Which hospital?' When Stephanie told him he asked quietly, 'He's going to be okay, right?'

It was Stephanie who answered. Of course it was. Kath seemed to have taken a step back on this job.

'He's the doctor and he didn't argue when I mentioned possible surgery.'

She could be sassy when she put her mind to it.

Jock was watching her far too closely. Would he remember briefly seeing her once, when they were knocking around together? Yeah, he would.

The man had a phenomenal memory—especially for trivia. He also didn't bother keeping things to himself if he knew he could rile his mates. But today Jock had better keep his big mouth shut or they'd be having words.

Pain stabbed in his thigh. He'd been focused on Jock and had moved without thinking. 'Let's get this show on the road,' he grunted to Kath.

She nodded back. 'I'll drive, Steph.'

A hint of pink streamed into Stephanie's cheeks. Had she been in the driving seat on the way here?

'Sure.' The finger on his pulse wobbled.

He could only hope her counting skills were still in good working order.

'See you at the hospital,' Jock called as the back doors closed.

'Sure,' he muttered, unable to deny the relief he felt that his pal would be hanging out with him in ED. Not that he wasn't capable of facing hassles alone. He was used to it. It was just that he didn't want to. Having a friend there when he felt like something the dog had regurgitated was what it was all about.

He even wished Stephanie still worked in the emergency department so she could stop by his cubicle occasionally until he was taken into Theatre. Because that was where he was headed.

Being a doctor didn't make that any less daunting than it would be for any other patient. The op wouldn't be major, but he'd still have to be anaesthetised. Not something that excited him. He hated being out of control. Once that drug sent him to sleep he wouldn't know another thing until the anaesthetist brought him round again—if he woke up.

Another shudder and goosebumps lifted the skin on his arms. If only they could fix him up using a local anaesthetic so he could be aware of everything happening…

'Lie down,' Stephanie ordered in that no-nonsense voice she was very good at with recalcitrant patients. 'You'll rock around too much if you're sitting, and that would not be good.' Then that toffee gaze locked onto his. 'Please?' she asked softly.

His heart slowed as he looked into those brown depths. Concern radiated out of them. She cared. For *him*. He wasn't just another patient to her. Warmth stole through his shaky body, flattened the goosebumps. For the life of him he couldn't banish the sense of wonder at the thought of being special to someone—if he only had the courage to become involved without looking for the divorce at the end of it.

He didn't want to be alone any more.

Which was scary—scarier than going under an anaesthetic.

No doubt it was all to do with post-accident

shock. Had to be. Any other explanation was untenable.

'Michael? Are you all right?'

Stephanie shook him gently—this time as a paramedic, not a friend.

'Look at me.'

'I'll need help lifting my leg onto the stretcher.'

Could she possibly do that without touching him? Not even those gloves were protecting him from the warm sensation of her fingertips on his skin.

Blimey, could she be gentle… It hurt like stink to lift his leg and swivel his butt so he could lie down, but Stephanie didn't add to his agony. Not at the site of his injuries anyway.

When Michael was wheeled into a room on the men's surgical ward three hours later, feeling as though a bus had run him over and with a mouth drier than a drought, relief at being awake overwhelmed him. The anaesthetic hadn't got him. Things were going his way. Plus the head nurse had given him a room to himself. Sometimes there were advantages to working in the hospital.

'Up for a beer, mate?' Jock strolled in, hands in his pockets, worry darkening his gaze, followed by Max, the other third of his lucky threesome.

So much for peace and quiet.

He smiled. 'Sure.'

He and these guys went way back, to their first day of high school, and there wasn't much they didn't know about each other.

'Shouldn't you be at the rugby?'

'Shucks, I knew we had to be somewhere else,' Jock quipped.

'You're missing the game of the season to hang out with *me*?'

'Nah, it doesn't start for another hour. We're foregoing the beers to check on you.'

'Find me some clothes and I'll come with you.'

'Did I just hear what I thought I did?'

In walked Stephanie, looking frazzled yet cute in tight black jeans and a fitted red jersey that highlighted her dark blonde hair perfectly.

'Depends how good your hearing is,' answered Jock, before Michael could come up with an answer.

His brain had been in slow mode since he'd come round in Recovery. Probably just as well, or he'd have made some smart aleck comment to keep the guys from seeing how much she got to him. And they'd have seen right through it.

Not that he couldn't enjoy lying there quietly watching her. She'd brushed her hair so it sat around her head with tantalising effect. As for that jersey—it highlighted each and every curve of her delightful breasts and narrow waist. Breasts and waist which he had no trouble recalling…could almost feel against the palms of his hands.

'How did the surgery go?' Stephanie stepped closer, a frown between her brows.

'I haven't talked to Chris yet,' he managed to croak over his even drier tongue.

'Chris Stuart operated?' The frown relaxed. 'He's the best.' Then she smiled and stepped away. 'I'll leave you to talk nonsense with your friends.'

But you just got here.

'Ignore them. They can talk amongst themselves.'

'No, I need to hit the supermarket.'

Supermarkets didn't close till ten at the earliest.

'Fair enough.'

He should be glad she wasn't going to hang about. *He wasn't.* Reaching for the water bottle on the bedside table, he groaned as murky pain reminded him of why he was there.

Instantly Stephanie picked up the bottle and handed it to him. 'Dry mouth? Anaesthetic will do that.'

Gulping mouthfuls of the cool liquid made him feel slightly more normal.

'Glad to see you're not lonely in here.'

Chris Stuart stood in the doorway.

'It's busier than the downtown train station at

rush hour,' Michael muttered. 'But at least I'll have a ride home with someone.'

'That'll be tomorrow at the earliest.' Chris came to stand at the end of the bed. 'You're post-op and unable to get around. No way you're going home tonight. Not even to stay with one of this lot.'

'Why? There weren't any complications?'

'No, all's good, but you won't be walking on that leg for a few days. The wound was serious. Your femur was nicked. Get the picture?'

Chris raised an eyebrow, which Michael ignored, not liking where this was going.

'That wrist needs resting too.' Chris held his hand up, palm outward, as Michael went to make a retort. 'You're no longer a gung-ho rugby player. You're more than ten years older than when you used to run around the rugby paddock.'

'Have you finished writing me off? Should I be buying a unit in the old folks' home?'

Chris grinned. 'If you want to get around without too much trouble in the future you'll do as I say.'

'Good luck with that,' Stephanie muttered. 'He walked to the ambulance earlier.'

'Now, *there's* a surprise.' Chris was enjoying giving him a stir-up. 'Hi, Steph. Didn't know you were back in town. How's things?'

'Good so far.'

So far? What was she expecting to go wrong? 'You're back in the ED?"

Now his pals were listening in, their ears like radar shields on a roof.

'I'm a paramedic on the ambulances now,' Steph told the nosy surgeon. 'Which is how come I got to bring *this* ungrateful man in for you to fix up.'

Max started laughing. 'She doesn't take any of your crap. I like her already.'

He didn't *have* to like her. She wasn't a part of their scene—didn't know their wives or kids, and wasn't going to. But he couldn't be down and out rude.

'Stephanie Roberts, meet another scoundrel— Max. We've been mates for ever.' And before Chris could add his piece he went on. 'I'll manage on my own at home'

But no one was listening. The other three men in the room were focused on Stephanie as she answered Chris's questions about where she'd been over the last couple of years.

'Now I'm home for good.' Her gaze drifted in his direction, flicked back to a spot on the floor in front of her.

'Since you're unencumbered, *you* could move in with Michael until he's back on his feet. Better than having him hanging around our place, where the baby is bound to keep him awake at night.' Smugness rolled off Jock as he showed his true colours.

'No!' Stephanie shook her head abruptly.

'Hang on, I—' Michael tried.

'That's a *great* idea,' said Chris. 'If you did that, Steph, I'd be happy to discharge Michael tomorrow morning, after I've checked him out. Otherwise I'll have to keep him in for a few days. He'll overdo things if he's on his own.'

'Sorry, but I go to work—night and day shifts. I wouldn't be there all the time.' She was almost pleading. 'And I've got a dog.'

'A dog *and* Mike?' Max grinned. 'Perfect.'

'The dog loves digging holes in the garden.' Steph sounded desperate.

Michael tried again. 'It's okay. I don't need you there.'

'We wouldn't have to worry about him,' Jock added. 'Or go round to make sure he hasn't fallen on his face.'

Definitely not a *friend*.

'Hello? I *am* here.'

Chris laughed. 'Annoying, aren't they?'

'Who needs friends when I've got these guys in my face?'

Jock stopped laughing and turned to Stephanie—and Michael knew. She was lost before she'd even got started. Which meant so was he. His mate was about to work his lawyering magic on her and she wouldn't be able to beat him at his game.

He sank back into the pillows and waited. This was going to be good—even if he would be the ultimate loser.

'Here's the thing, Steph. Mike's more than welcome to come stay with me and my family, but he won't. He's stubborn like that—won't want to be a nuisance.'

Stephanie's face was a picture as it dawned on her that she was on a road to nowhere. She was a quick learner. The colour in her cheeks ebbed away as her gaze remained on his mate's face.

'Mike won't go to Max's for the same reason. He will go home alone, regardless what any of us want,' Jock continued. 'I concede that he doesn't want you with him, any more than you want him to be there, but he wants out of here ASAP so it *is* the best option.'

'Maybe for Michael, but not for me,' she whispered.

Michael silently applauded her valiant effort, all the while knowing it wouldn't make a jot of difference.

'Give me a moment,' said Jock, in that take-no-prisoners voice that won him court case after court case. 'You're a nurse, right?'

Close enough. Once a nurse always a nurse.

This could go on for hours, and in the end he and Stephanie were going to lose anyway. There

was a gloating gleam in his pal's eyes that would
take a bomb to shift. Which meant he had to give
in, didn't he?

'Give up, Stephanie. Jock's not going to let up
until you fold. We'll make it work.'

He'd almost stopped breathing, watching her,
thinking about that kiss. He would make it work
for both of them. Or die trying.

Stunned eyes turned in his direction. 'You
want me to move in temporarily?'

No. But if not her then who? Because the only
way he was getting out of here was with someone
at home to run around after him. There was no
alternative. None that he'd *like*, that was.

'Two days. That's all it'll take for me to get
mobile enough to look after myself. As you said,
you'll be working most of the time. These oafs
can check in on me occasionally.'

'Which kind of negates me staying with you,'
she snapped, desperate to the end.

'I get that.'

It was hard to know what was eating at him
the most: the fact she didn't want to stay with
him or the unexpected hope that she'd capitulate.
He didn't want her in his house, where he could
see her and hear that soft, sweet voice too much,
where that honey scent of hers would permeate
the rooms, the air, everything. But if *anyone* had
to sit in his lounge and eat takeaways with him
then Stephanie was his pick.

'What if I promise not to move all day while you're at work?'

Left corner rising... Then her mouth straightened again. 'There are complications with that—unless you get a potty from ED.' Her nose wrinkled in that funny, cute way.

'I can keep your dog company—make sure he's not lonely and digging where he shouldn't. All from my chair, of course.'

'Why have you changed—?' She stopped, swallowed and drew a deep breath.

The room was suddenly silent, and sounds from the ward outside infiltrated as everyone waited for Stephanie to continue. Michael could feel his lungs tightening as he held his breath. Having her in his house wasn't going to be easy, but having her stick to her guns was starting to rile him. He was flat-out annoyed that she didn't want to spend time with him.

He must have hit his head when he went down, because none of this was making sense.

'I'll do it.'

It was barely a whisper crossing her lips, but he heard each word clearly, felt each one on his skin like a light summer breeze coming off the sea.

'Thank you.'

Best leave it at that, or she might change her mind. It was suddenly imperative she didn't. Which meant he should be booking into a hotel for the next week—not going to his house—paying a nurse to come in and change his dressings—not letting this one near him. Because Stephanie Roberts had sneaked in under his skin once more and now he had to be extra-vigilant. He was not getting involved with her. Not, not, *not*.

'I'll text you when Chris lets me loose.'

He chose to ignore the gleeful grins on his mates' faces. They could get lost as well.

Stephanie was still looking stunned at what she'd agreed to. 'What about your sister?' she croaked. 'We could ask her to help.'

Max cut her off. 'Chantelle and medical dressings? Don't go there. You're it for as long as Mike needs you.'

Max had made that up about Chantelle. 'Haven't you got a game to go watch?' Michael growled.

That got them moving. The clock was ticking, and in their haste to set him up they'd forgotten they had yet to confront the traffic that would be clogging the roads around Eden Park.

'We've got a spare ticket to the rugby. Chris?'

'Give me five and I'll be right with you. I'm all done here for the rest of the night. Thanks, Stephanie. Word of warning: your services will be required for at least three days.' He grinned. 'Thanks for the ticket, Michael.'

Michael glared at his surgeon. 'Any time you

want to go let me know and I'll find another axe to do some damage with.'

'Is there a television on the ward?' his new housemate wondered in the sudden silence that fell after the three wise asses had left.

'There'll be one in the lounge at the far end.'

Though the prospect of getting out of bed to go along there was not exciting him.

'I could watch on my phone if I had it with me.'

It had been in his pocket when he'd chopped himself, which had saved him hauling his butt around the house looking for it to call for help. But where it had got to was anyone's guess.

Pity, because he really wanted to watch the game from the comfort of this bed. Negotiating crutches or a wheelchair did not appeal now the codeine was lightening off. Taking another pill could wait until he was ready to sleep. Drugs were all very well, but they made him groggy and he preferred to go minimal where he could on that score.

'That'd drive you bonkers, wouldn't it? With such a tiny screen you'd struggle to see it clearly.'

She looked at him hard and saw his frustration.

'You phoned for an ambulance, so I'm figuring you dropped the phone on your porch afterwards.'

'Hope I haven't had any unwanted visitors

since then.' Losing his phone would be more than a nuisance, with all the numbers he had stored.

'I'll go get it. Anything else you want? Clothes to go home in? Toothbrush?'

He nodded. 'All of those. Jock dropped my keys on the bedside table.'

Thank goodness one of them had been alert. He hadn't given it a thought. Anaesthetic brain had a lot to answer for.

'Steph, I'm sorry to be a pain.'

She blinked. 'It's okay.'

He'd called her Steph. Letting go of another knot that kept her that little bit removed from him. Anaesthetic brain again.

'You might want to bring my car when you come to collect me. I'm not likely to get this leg into your matchbox.' It would really give him grief if he tried folding it up to his chin.

'No problem. I'd better fly. Kick-off's in forty.'

She snatched up his house keys and disappeared before he had time to answer. Everyone seemed to be leaving him in a hurry today.

CHAPTER SIX

To wake him or not? The game started in five.

Steph eased onto the chair beside Michael's hospital bed and gazed at his face, free of pain and tension in sleep. Still as handsome, still making her blood heat. *Michael.* How had she thought she could get over him? Despite the years since she'd last touched him her palms could still feel the sensation of that warm skin, of his hard muscles. More important, she still knew the hope he brought her for a future of love.

There was no answer as to why it was Michael over other men she'd known. It was what it was. Attraction, both physical and mental. So deep that hope was an integral part of her, and finally she understood that removing it would be as impossible as whipping out her liver or kidneys. No cure available.

But right now he wouldn't thank her if he missed the game—even if he did need to sleep.

'Michael,' she called softly.

She needed to hand over his gear and get out of

there to digest what she'd let herself in for. Days and nights with Michael, in his house, looking after him. How had *that* happened?

She'd been conned, that was how. By a smart guy looking out for his friend. She couldn't argue with that, even when the arguments were stacking up in her head. It was exactly what Jill would've done for her.

'Michael,' she tried, a bit louder, keen to get away.

When he didn't stir she leaned across and laid her hand on his upper arm, shook gently.

'It's kick-off time.'

'What?' His eyes opened, closed again.

'The rugby, Michael.'

This time his eyelids lifted and stayed up. 'You got my phone?'

'And the other things you wanted. But I thought this would be better to watch the game.' She passed over her tablet. 'Larger screen.'

He reached for the tablet—with the wrong hand. His groan was deep, throaty, and the pain from that sprained wrist showed in his face.

'Easy…'

Using only one arm made his shuffling upright an awkward struggle, and a sheen of sweat broke out on his forehead.

Steph plumped the pillows behind his back, gently pushed him into them before turning on the tablet and finding the game.

'Want to stay and watch with me?'

Pardon? Was he serious? Or not thinking straight?

'I don't think we can both watch on that tiny screen.'

In other words, No, I do not. We're going to be spending too much time together starting to-morrow.

'We'll manage.' He slid sideways and patted the bed. 'Here.'

You're kidding, right?

How was she supposed to do that without getting in a fever? But it seemed her heart had taken charge, because she was soon parked beside him, staring at the screen. Not looking anywhere else, not breathing, not feeling his arm against hers. Totally unaware of him.

Pants on fire.

The game had started. 'Go, you idiot, *run*!' Michael almost shouted as one of the Auckland forwards stole the ball from the opposition. 'Look out!'

'Shh, you're in a hospital ward,' she nudged him. 'Some people in here are sick.'

He totally ignored her. 'What sort of pass was that?'

Steph went to close the door. This was not going to be a quiet eighty minutes, so she'd minimise the damage. Then the game pulled her in and she forgot where she was, and even who she was squashed up against—okay, that was an exaggeration—until, in frustration at a player's move, Michael slapped his hand down on his thigh.

'Ahhh!'

The sound of raw pain drowned out the commentators and the background noise of the shouting crowd.

Standing up, Steph lifted his hand away from his leg and checked the dressing. 'Got to watch out.'

His breathing was shallow and rapid, his good hand a fist, his face white.

She gripped his hand in both hers, held him until the tension eased from his muscles and his eyes opened.

'Don't say a word,' he growled. 'I've got more than enough cuss words of my own.'

Focusing on the screen, he drew in long, soothing lungsful of air, hissing them out again over tight lips.

When Steph tried to free her hands from his he turned his hand to hold on to her. She went with it, as it was one way to prevent him doing anything so mindless again.

Sitting back on the bed, not so close as to be touching his arm, hip and thigh this time, she did some breathing exercises of her own to lessen the tension cramping her stomach, her chest… her sex. Being this close to him was hard, not touching him even more so—but extremely wise and safe.

But it might not be the case by the time she moved out of Michael's house in a few days.

'Come and get me, will you? Before Chris changes his mind. I've had enough of this place and people poking thermometers in my mouth and shining torches in my face all night long. How's a bloke supposed to recover when they don't let him sleep?'

Michael was grumpy.

'And don't forget to bring my car. I'm not tying myself in knots getting into that miniscule thing you drive.'

'Yes, sir.'

Great. Steph sighed into her tea. The man was belligerent as all get out.

'I'll be about an hour.'

'An *hour*? The hospital's just down the road, woman. I need to get out of here. *Now.*'

'Anyone would think you're in jail,' she retorted. 'I have to go to the supermarket to get Zac some biscuits first. Might get you some too.'

She'd been intending to go to the vet's, but judging by the angst coming through the phone that would have to go on hold. It was going to be difficult enough spending the day with him, without having a bad mood hovering between them.

'Pick me up first. I'll sit in the car while you

shop,' he said, and followed up with a grunt. 'Please.'

That was all it took. 'Please' spoken in that husky tone and she was his. *Ah, no.* Okay, she'd oblige him in this but nothing else. That was better.

'Do you mind if Zac comes for the ride?'

'Buckle him into Aaron's seat.'

Was that a laugh? Couldn't be. 'Yeah, right.'

Actually, it wasn't such a bad idea—if only Zac was a little bit smaller. She'd seen the injuries inflicted on a front passenger by a dog in the back seat slamming forward when a truck took out the car it was in. As for the dog... She shuddered, glad she hadn't seen that.

'I'll be waiting at the main entrance.'

Michael hung up on her, clearly convinced she would swing by for him before doing anything else.

As tempting as it was to make him wait, she didn't. One: that temper of his would only increase, which wasn't the way to start their days sharing his house. It was going to be strained enough. Two: he was still recovering from surgery and needed to be at home, where it was warm and comfortable, not sitting in a busy vestibule being knocked and nudged by people coming and going.

When she pulled up he was sitting on a bench outside the hospital in the cold wind, looking pale and uncomfortable. There was no wheel-chair in sight—only a crutch that had fallen to the ground by his feet.

'Hey,' Steph said as she opened the passenger door. 'How did you get down here?'

'There's this thing called a lift.'

The way he was struggling to stand up made her want to shake him—hard. He didn't have to put himself through any more pain than neces-sary.

Swallowing her anger, she moved to take his elbow and wrap an arm around his waist. 'Come on. Get in the car.'

Michael sagged against her, giving away how much he was hurting. 'Bossy creature, aren't you?'

'You'd better believe it.'

As quickly as her anger had risen it faded away. He was a man who believed in being tough, strong, inviolate. Face it: she wouldn't be interested in a wimp. But did he have to be so stubborn?

It took some effort to get Michael into his car, but with a few curses on his side and determi-nation and care on hers he was finally installed, looking even paler and gulping air as if it was going out of fashion fast.

Zac settled his snout on Michael's shoulder, and didn't seem perturbed that he wasn't ac-knowledged.

'Stephanie?'

Michael tapped her hand until she looked at him.

'Thank you. For everything. I know you aren't keen to stay with me, so you need to know I appreciate it.'

Not what she'd expected. 'It's fine.' She pulled out into the traffic. 'Maybe I should take you home first...get you settled.'

His chest rose and fell. 'No, I'm okay.' Tipping his head sideways, he watched her watching the road. 'Truly. It's no more uncomfortable sitting in here than it will be at home. Let's get whatever you need first.'

'Fine. On your head be it. Is there anything you want? I'm warning you: cooking is not my forte.'

With his regular list of takeout menus he was safe for the few nights she'd be there, because getting involved in a kitchen and a pantry was *not* happening.

'How much not your thing?'

'I can boil vegetables, heat soup, put a casserole together with the help of a recipe.'

That wasn't so bad.

'Oh, and make toast.'

'Want to pick up some soup? And a ham bone in case I get creative in the coming days.'

Suddenly Steph laughed. 'This is nuts. Here we are, two supposedly intelligent people, planning a meal out of a can. Maybe it's time I put an effort into cooking. Roasts and steak and sticky date puddings.'

'You like sticky date too?'

He smacked those delicious lips.

'I'll book you in for a cookery course tomorrow.' Then, 'How come your mum didn't teach you the basics?'

'She tried, but I always wanted to be outside with my brothers. They did cool stuff, like climb trees and build huts, ride cycle tracks. Who would want to be stuck inside when they could do all that?'

'You were married. Still no cooking?'

'Some—nothing fancy.' Another thing Freddy had finally come to grizzle about, even though it hadn't been an issue in the beginning.

The supermarket car park was almost empty. She pulled up close to the front and leapt out.

'Back in a tick.'

She raced up and down the aisles, lifting cans, bread and chocolate, and dog biscuits. She whipped through the self check-out and tossed her bag on the seat beside Zac.

She needn't have bothered rushing. Michael's head was tipped back, his eyes closed, and his breathing light. It was a silent few minutes driving from the supermarket to his house.

'Someone's been here,' she commented, more to herself than to her two companions, as she parked as close to the front door as possible to save Michael any more walking than necessary. Smoke was billowing out of the chimney.

Michael came awake instantly. 'Max said he'd drop by…make himself useful.'

'Wait there while I open the door and dump these bags.' She also let Zac out, and he immediately bounded across to a lemon tree to cock his leg.

'I like your new housemate. We had quite the discussion while you were shopping,' Michael commented when she returned to help him out of the car. He was keeping a wary eye on the dog, with his injured leg furthest away from that solid head.

'You were faking that sleep?'

He hadn't budged when she'd shut her door and started up the engine.

'Zac, sit.' He instantly obeyed. Unbelievable. 'Good boy. He's been an angel so far—apart from the holes he dug—so I'm hoping he'll be well-behaved here.'

Winding her arm around Michael's waist she helped him inside with his other arm hanging over her shoulder. Occasionally, when his leg dragged or knocked a step, his fingers dug hard.

'Relax. I don't mind having Zac here. Sometimes I think I should get a dog myself. Aaron would love it. But my hours don't lend enough time.'

He made it right through to the kitchen and dropped onto a chair with a wince and a groan. The crutch clattered against the table and slid to the floor, sending Zac skittering backwards as he stared at the noisy thing.

Placing the crutch out of the way, but close enough for Michael to reach, Steph admitted, 'That's my big concern about Zac. That he'll be lonely while I'm at work. So I'm going to enquire about getting a minder. Someone who'll take him for walks on those days.'

'There's a guy who does it for some of the hospital staff. He'll keep your dog at his place all day, if necessary. Ask the Radiology crowd. At least two of them use his services and they swear by him.'

'That's brilliant.' The guilt niggling at her since she'd decided to keep Zac disappeared. 'I wonder if this guy would drop by and check up on *you* while I'm at work. He could even take you for a hop around the park on your crutch.'

Michael glared at her. 'Woof, woof.'

'Know any good dog food takeout places?'

'Watch it.'

Opening the fridge to put away the butter and milk, she gaped. 'Someone's been busy. There's a casserole in here.'

'That'll be Max's wife. She's always baking and cooking. Believes it's the way to everyone's heart.' He made to push up off his seat and immediately dropped down again. 'Aaron's more nimble than I am at the moment.'

'Which is why I've been coerced into staying here. What are you wanting?'

'You can leave any time you like. It wasn't me who twisted your arm.'

'Your pal was very persuasive. And neither did you really add any weight at the end. I might've resisted otherwise.'

She still wasn't certain she'd done the right thing, coming here.

'Do you want coffee?'

He nodded. 'I was trying to make it easier for you to give in without Jock gloating. He's good at that. But seriously, Steph, if you don't want to be here then please go back to your place. I won't be offended.'

So she was Steph today as well? Still sounded sexy on his tongue.

'Which room do I use?'

Yours? Do I get to share your bed?

She'd had her chance two nights ago and run.

'Take your pick—though Aaron usually goes in the one next to mine when he's staying, so I can hear him if he wakes.' Michael grimaced.

'Does Chantelle know about your operation?'

'Max phoned her first thing this morning, just as she was going into a lecture.'

'Where's Aaron?'

'In the university crèche since it was only for

an hour. Strange she didn't try to drop him off at my place. He won't be staying here for a few days now. I couldn't keep up with him.'

'So what will Chantelle do about that?'

Steph searched the cupboards for mugs and coffee.

'Learn to take care of things herself.'

'Come on. From what you told me she's already doing that.'

Leaning back against the bench, she crossed her ankles and waited for him to answer. *If* he answered.

'Your brothers don't give you any grief about the things you choose to do?'

Where had that come from?

'None at all. Growing up, we were one big happy family and nothing's really changed. Except my best friend is now my sister-in-law, which is cool.'

'As long as nothing goes wrong.'

Steph stared at Michael. 'Wow, that's negative.'

'What would happen to your friendship if your brother's marriage failed? Would you and your friend remain on good terms?'

'I don't see why not. Now that time's passed I get on with my ex whenever I bump into him.'

Michael's eyebrows rose. 'Really? That's unusual.'

'So I'm told. Sugar?'

'One. How often do you see Freddy?'

He sounded…jealous? *Nah*—that would be ridiculous.

'Not for a while since I've been away.'

Coffee splashed over her fingers as she vigorously stirred sugar into both mugs.

'Here.'

After sliding one onto the table, she headed into the lounge to check if the fire needed more wood. It didn't.

'Jock can't have left here much before we got home.'

Michael was watching her as she returned to her coffee. 'I was married once.'

What was this? One confidence for another?

'I'm sorry it didn't work out.'

I am not asking why, but I'd like to know.

'So was I, at the time.' He sipped his coffee. 'But in retrospect the chances of it working out were probably fifty-fifty at best. We weren't ideally suited in many respects.'

'How old were you?'

What had happened to not asking anything?

His smile was self-deprecating. 'Twenty-two. We married while I was still playing rugby. Divorced when I began packing in the hours studying at med school.'

'That's young. I met Freddy while I was training. He's nearly ten years older and was getting established in private practice as a plastic surgeon.'

'Where is he working now?'

'On the North Shore.'

The coffee was too strong.

'What do you want me to get organised before I leave for work at five?'

'This is why I argued with Chris. I don't need any help. I can turn the oven on...put that casserole in to heat.'

'Changing your dressings might be difficult.' Steph fidgeted with her mug.

'Can't you do that before you leave? I'll take a shower first. It's been a while and I feel grubby. They sure know how to ramp up the heat on the ward.'

'Newsflash: a shower is out of the question. Wrapping plastic around your thigh to prevent water seeping through won't work.'

'Yes, Nurse,' he said grumpily. 'I hate it when you're right. I'll run a bath, then, keep this leg hanging over the edge.'

Oh, boy. This just got worse and worse. 'How are you going to lower yourself into the water with only one hand? And—' she waved her finger in front of him '—how are you going to get out again when you can't put any weight on that leg?'

'You're enjoying this.'

'Absolutely not.' And she was not seeing him

naked on anyone's watch. Then again, neither was Michael falling and doing more damage on her watch.

Oh, boy, now what?

'Between us, I'll get in and out of the bath without too much hassle.'

His jaw clenched. He obviously knew it was going to hurt, but what was the alternative?

'I can give you a sponge-down. A warm cloth and soapy water is just as effective as a shower or bath.' *And less revealing.* No need to remove his boxers. He could sit on a stool with towels on the floor while she washed that skin, felt those muscles under her fingertips, tried to ignore his body.

But Michael was shaking his head. Of course he was. Stubborn man. Infuriating man.

He would wash himself. He did not need Stephanie wiping his fevered skin, leaning close, her breath whispering across his body, that honey scent teasing his senses.

'I'm having a bath,' Michael reiterated.

He would banish her to the kitchen until he was ready to get out. If she hadn't already run out the front door.

Stephanie wouldn't run. She might feel uncomfortable, even angry with him, but she'd never shirk her duty. *Duty.* That was what he was to her today. A duty. She'd been coerced into helping him, and he had to take some of the flak for that. And if that was disappointment cloud-ing his thinking he only had himself to blame. But he'd throw his mates into the mix for good measure. No point in suffering alone.

Michael reached for his crutch and placed it straight up beside his injured leg. He pushed up-ward. The crutch slipped and he dropped back on the chair.

Deep breath...wait for the pain to ease off. Try again. Slip. Again.

The throbbing in his thigh increased expo-nentially.

'Stephanie.' Where had she gone? 'Steph!'

'Problem?' She appeared in the doorway. 'I've started running the bath.' Her gaze scanned him, hesitated on the hand clutching the useless crutch. 'Can't get up?'

'I'm being careful, okay?'

Down, man, down. This is not Steph's fault. And stop calling her Steph. It's too friendly.

'Can you give me a hand?'

Literally. Without saying a word. Without feel-ing soft and gentle and blood-thickeningly sen-sual.

If only she was as good at mind-reading as she was at nursing. That last memo clearly hadn't made it across to her head.

Her fingers brushed the back of his hand on their way to his elbow. Honey filled the air be-tween them and her hair gleamed under the overhead light. How had he walked away from this woman before he'd had his fill of that wondrous body?

Getting to his en suite bathroom was painful. His wrist throbbed like the devil, his thigh worse. The axe had gone as deep as his femur, and bone pain was ghastly.

He nearly stopped at his bed to spread out and let his body recoup. But he was determined to scrub up. His skin felt gross. He'd got a sweat up chopping wood before those cats had done their number on him. Throw in all those hours spent in one bed or another and he was in need of hot water and soap. Not gentle hands and caring eyes.

Dropping the crutch on the bathroom floor, he tugged his jersey and shirt over his head, swore when his sprained wrist got caught up in the sleeve.

'Let me.'

Stephanie was right there, untangling the fabric, carefully removing the sleeve. Not touching his skin. Then she started on the tape holding his wrist.

'Might as well take this off. It'll get soaked no matter how careful we are.'

'*We?* I'm having a bath. Not you.'

A blush rose in her cheeks. 'I have no intention of getting in with you. Just washing your back and your good arm since you won't be able to manage that.'

I don't think so.

Michael pushed his track pants down and stepped out of them.

That pink hue turned red as Stephanie stared at him.

Then he dropped his boxers and hopped over to the bath.

Forget red. Her cheeks were alight.

'You—' She swallowed hard. 'You could've kept them on.'

'Do you bathe in your underwear? When you want to clean yourself?' he taunted, in need of keeping her on her toes in case he lost it and grabbed her to him. Because he wanted to. Very much.

'No. But—' Another swallow.

'It's not as though you haven't seen it all before. You're a nurse.'

Not to mention their weeks together, when clothes hadn't been a part of what they'd got up to.

He parked his naked butt on the side of the bath and swung his good leg over into the water. So far so good. He lifted his injured leg. Rather, *tried* to lift it, and clenched his fists as pain whipped him.

Nurse Stephanie was instantly there, her hands

on his calf, carefully raising his leg to slide over the edge.

'Now you just have to lower your backside into the water without getting that wound wet.'

Clipped words, firm hands under his arm, pressed lips forcing all colour away.

Focusing entirely on getting into the bath and not swearing out loud, Michael finally managed to sit on the bottom and raise his injured leg to hang over the side.

'Thanks, Nurse. I'll manage now.'

Dismissed. Steph charged out of the bathroom, leaving the door open so she could hear if Michael called out.

It was tempting to head outside, take Zac for a walk—except it would be closer to a run before her anger calmed. She even picked up the lead from the bench.

Zac sat up, his tail wagging in anticipation.

'Sorry, my boy.' She dropped the lead and rubbed his ears. 'We can't leave him to get out of the bath on his own.'

How was she supposed to help him now? He needed his back and his arm washed. How to not notice everything about him? As in *everything*.

You've seen it all before.

Sure she had. She remembered his 'all'. It was the hot memories of that 'all' she couldn't deal with. This was the man she'd spent two years and thousands of kilometres trying to put behind her. Yet she'd reacted to his voice the first time he spoke to her at the beginning of the week.

Immediately she'd wanted to curl up against that expansive chest and feel as though she'd arrived at her destination. Her knees had melted when he'd kissed her—and, yes, she'd kissed him back.

But he didn't want her. Though she was beginning to think he *did* want her in his bed for a rerun of last time.

But he didn't *want*, want her. Not in his life, at his side, to be his partner, his wife. *His wife?* He'd reject her as sure as lightning came before thunder.

Again Steph snatched up the dog's lead. To hell with him. She had to get some air. Enough to keep her lungs working while her heart shut down and dealt with the pain stabbing at it.

'Stephanie? Can you wash my back?'

She froze. Totally. No heartbeat. No breathing. Dead but alive. Numb yet in pain.

Wife? That entailed love. Well, it did for her. This cramping sensation holding her, stuck, unable to move, was love. She'd screwed up bigtime.

'Steph?'

Play the friendship card, why don't you?

She was all out of them.

The lead banged onto the floor, snapping

her into action. Head up, lungs working, back straighter than a ruler, mind focused on the job. Wash his back, get him out of the bath without crashing to the floor, dry him off. *No way.* He could manage that part all by himself. He had to.

'Then we'll go for a walk,' she said, and patted Zac. 'After that I'll go to work and leave you with him. Sorry, but he won't upset you like he does me.'

Her resolve lasted until she reached the side of the bath. One glance at that muscular chest and she was lost. Her hand shook as she snatched the washcloth from him. The shaking became an earthquake as she sponged his back—right down to where his butt met the bottom of the bath.

How the hell was she supposed to get through the coming days?

She tried for an icy tone, instead got melted goo that made her sound like a drunk. 'Right, let's get you out of here.'

His skin was wet, and warm, and *so* tempting. *It's an arm.*

Her fingers dug deep.

Michael gripped the edge of the bath and shoved up, wobbling in circles as he strived for balance.

Being afraid he'd fall focused Steph on what she should have been concentrating on all along.

'Put your arm over my shoulder and use me as a crutch.'

And hurry up before I give in and turn to lay my face against your chest, to kiss you.

'Hey, Mike? You inside?' The question was followed by the front door slamming.

'Great timing,' Michael muttered as he reached for a towel. 'Chantelle?'

'Yes.'

He raised his voice. 'I'm getting out of the bath. Wait out there, will you?'

Steph fixed him with a look that said, *Your sister's probably seen it all before too, when you were kids.*

'You don't want her thinking we've got something going on between us, do you?' he asked.

'I don't give a damn.'

Yes, well. Brave words.

Judging by the cynicism on Michael's face he didn't believe her any more than she did herself.

'I'm here as a nurse who also happens to be a friend.' She winced over that one.

'Did you find the casserole I made?' Chantelle called from inside his bedroom.

'*You* made it?'

Steph pulled a face at his scepticism. 'Michael…' she whispered. 'Behave.'

He took the towel she held out and wrapped it around his waist. 'Sorry. Stephanie found it. I figured—'

Steph put her hand over his mouth, shook her head at him, whispered, 'Say thank you. *Nicely.*'

Then she removed her hand—but not before he'd breathed on her palm, sending her hormones into a riot of excitement.

'Thanks, Chantelle. What kind of casserole is it?' He raised an eyebrow at her, as if he was asking, *How am I doing?*

She smothered a smile and nodded.

'Uncle Mike—there you are!' A blur of arms and legs shot into the room.

Steph reacted instinctively to prevent the dynamo launching himself against his uncle's injury. Grabbing Aaron, she swung him up into her arms.

'Hi, Aaron. Remember me? Uncle Mike's friend Steph.'

'Friend? I thought you said she was a nurse,' Chantelle said as she appeared around the door.

'I want to hug Uncle Mike.' Aaron wriggled to be put down.

'You can when he's got dressed, okay?' Steph told him. 'Uncle Mike's hurt his leg, so you have to be very careful not to bump him.'

As if a three-year-old would take any notice.

Michael leaned towards his nephew, rubbed his head. 'I'll be with you in a minute, buddy, but you've got to go with Mum and Stephanie now.'

'No. I want *you.*'

'I'll be real fast. Promise.'

That was a promise he'd have trouble keeping in his condition. And she wasn't thinking about his sculpted chest or saucy butt. Well, she *was*, but not in terms of his promise.

'I'll put the kettle on.'

As if *that* was going to help—but it was what her grandmother had always done when she hadn't known what to do about a situation. Besides, a cup of tea wouldn't go astray. Her nerves needed help calming down.

'You're not going to help Michael finish drying off and get him dressed?' Chantelle asked, with a wicked glint in her eyes.

'He's quite capable.' Though she would have helped if his sister hadn't turned up. 'I'll just grab some clean clothes for him.'

Which meant going through his drawers. How personal was *that*? How soon could she leave for work?

CHAPTER SEVEN

ZAC GREETED STEPH with a wagging tail when she crawled out of her car at Michael's place just after six-thirty the next morning. 'Hey, my boy, good to see you too. Who let you out?'

The house was eerily quiet.

She tiptoed through to the kitchen on legs that must have done a thousand kilometres throughout her shift, her mind filled with images of a boy racer's car wrapped around a power pole, its drunk occupants tossed across the bonnet oblivious to the sirens and people stemming bloodflow and buckling on neck braces. The ambulance crews had taken two of the boys to the ED, while a low black saloon had transported a third to the morgue.

Her stomach cramped in hunger. Eggs on toast would be heaven, and might make up for the couple of snatched mouthfuls of a cruddy dry sandwich in the crew kitchen hours ago, but pouring muesli out of a box was a lot quicker, with no thought processes required.

It was already too crowded in her skull, with images of those kids refusing to go away, vying with Michael for attention. He'd been there in her thoughts all night, only backing off when total concentration had been needed for her patients, returning the moment she was free. The man had a way of making her feel as though her feet were on ice, sending her in every direction but the one she'd intended going.

How to make him go away, leave her in peace, when she did not need him interfering with her life plans?

But he refused to go away.

He was such a distraction.

Like sitting naked in the bath while she washed his back and almost put a tooth through her bottom lip as she denied the need to wash more, touch more. Like talking to her as though this was normal—which it could be if they were in a real relationship. Like being so relaxed with her when she was tighter than a triple knot in comparison.

If ever there was a man she could envisage spending her life with he was… Michael.

She'd known it for a long time. Throughout all those hours, days months and years she'd spent running, trying to bury him in the back of her mind, he had still been under her skin, still heating her blood, still meaning everything to her. He still sent her heart into a whacky rhythm.

So much for thinking she was an intelligent woman.

Sanity.

Highly overrated.

She obviously didn't have any.

Michael Laing ruled her heart. Someone had to as she was obviously incapable.

'Morning. You look like you had the night from hell.'

As Michael crashed into her reverie for real Steph tripped over her feet and stared at him as if he was a stranger.

'Why are you up? Didn't you sleep well?'

There were deep shadows smeared across his cheekbones, but only mild pain in his eyes. Plus a dose of resignation. What was *that* about?

'I prefer those nights where I don't know a thing until the alarm goes off,' he admitted. 'Want a cup of tea? Unless you've changed your morning fix?'

He remembered. 'I'll get it. You stay put.' He wasn't putting weight on that leg for her. 'Want one?'

'Please. And can you wake Chantelle? She needs to get up and sort Aaron or she'll be late for work. Oh, and Zac's outside in the back yard. He was crossing his legs when I came out here half an hour ago.'

'I received my good morning nudge the moment I stepped out of my car.' And then she'd shut the door on him, focused on not waking Michael. 'What sort of doggy mother am I?' Opening the back door she called, 'Zac? Where are you, boy?'

A black and tan form charged her, skidded to a halt at her feet, a big head bumping her. Wag, wag, went that thick tail.

A lump filled her throat as she leaned down to rub Zac's head, then his back. Already she was smitten. *Oh, come on.* She'd been lost from the first pat she'd given him. Like with Michael. The first day he'd arrived in the ED to start his contract she'd been hooked. Their first kiss had had her falling for him.

Yeah, she'd always been in love with him. It was how all her important relationships had started. She and Jill had known from their first morning on the school mat that they were best pals. Freddy much the same—if not on the school mat. If ever she'd needed proof that she wasn't going to get over Michael now she had it.

But she already knew that.

Steph sighed and nuzzled her face against Zac's neck. 'How come you're so quick to trust me?' It didn't say a lot for his affection for his previous owner. Or did it mean the other woman's love had taught him there were only kind people out there?

'He whimpers a lot in his sleep.'

She'd forgotten how near Michael was.

'I think he does miss his other home, but he's very happy with you. Sucks up love and attention like a sponge,' he added.

'Strange how he turned up at my house and never left. He was there every time I went home. Why, boyo? Did you sense I'd buy you sirloin once week as a treat?'

'What's not to trust about you, Steph?'

'I used to be a flight risk.' Standing up, she ran a hand over her messy hair. 'I ran out of Auckland when you finished with me. Then I left Queenstown when the two girls I worked with fell in love and had babies. As for London and Europe—I could never stay in one place for very long. The moment things seemed to be going great I'd find something to be unhappy about.'

Michael flinched. 'But you're home for good this time, right?'

'I am. No matter what happens here, this is where I belong. It's about the only thing I'm sure of some days.'

She closed the back door to keep the early-morning cold at bay and headed to the bench and that tea she was supposed to be making.

Oops, Chantelle needed rousing.

'As long as I can keep that at the front of my mind,' she muttered as she headed down the hall, 'and not let the fear of being dumped again get in the way.'

* * *

So she loved Michael. She really loved him. Trying to get over him was never going to work. And with her being back here, now she needed a new plan.

A deep breath made her lungs sting. Go after him. Woo him. Show him how she felt. Prove her love was real and honest and for ever.

Steph sagged against the wall. Could she do that? Her heart was already Michael's, so what was there to lose?

'Steph? You okay?' Chantelle stood in front of her.

Great. Now Michael's sister would have the wrong impression of her.

'I'm fine. I was coming to wake you up, but seems I wasn't needed.'

'Michael won't believe I'm capable of setting an alarm.' It was said with a smile but there was weariness in her voice. 'He's a work in progress when it comes to trusting me to live my life without mishaps.'

'He wants the best for you.'

Steph had seen the surprise in Michael's eyes when Chantelle had rung yesterday to say she'd stay the night here in case he needed help getting about. That surprise had been replaced with relief, showing how worried he'd been about being on his own.

'If I didn't know that I'd have left town years

ago.' Chantelle opened Aaron's door, glanced over her shoulder to Steph. 'How *is* Grumpy Socks this morning?'

'Sitting in the kitchen looking tired. Did you have to get up for him during the night?' Steph asked.

Chantelle grinned. 'What do you think? This is Michael we're talking about—self-sufficient and always giving help, never asking for any.'

Steph huffed. 'Should've known.'

His sister stared at her. 'How well do you know him? I thought you— It doesn't matter.'

Was that disappointment in her eyes? Why? For what?

'We worked together for a couple of years a while back, so I know him well professionally.'

Which meant she knew his stalwart character, his kindness, gentleness, his concern for people in dire situations.

'So why are you here now? This isn't a work environment, even if he does need your nursing skills.'

Good question—and one she still wasn't ready to answer out loud. 'He begged. I folded.'

'Michael begged?' Chantelle stared at her, her mouth widening into an infuriating grin. 'My brother *begged* you to help him out?'

Uh-oh. Trouble lurking.

'His mates were pushing me to acquiesce. I

think Michael asked me to stay over just to shut them down.'

Take that on board and smoke it.

'You mean Max and Jock?' Chantelle nodded. 'That I can believe. I also know exactly what they're up to. You so don't know what you've got yourself into. You're fried!'

'Mummy, I want Bugsy.'

Saved by the boy. Once more. She owed him an ice cream.

'I'll get that tea I've been trying to make for the last ten minutes.'

Michael was at the bench, his hip propped against it, dropping teabags into mugs. 'Chantelle in a good mood?'

A scheming one. 'Why wouldn't she be?'

'She gets tired with Aaron and studying, and doesn't always show how happy she is.' He filled the mugs with boiling water.

'Go and sit down. I'll get these.' Steph nudged him with an elbow.

Michael caught her arm, tugged her to face him. 'I know you didn't want to be here with me, so thanks again. I'm trying not to be a pain in the backside.'

Instant heat flared in her arm, sending sparks of desire along her arm. Not want to be with him? Wrong. She definitely wanted to be here. What she didn't need was getting in a pickle over the sexual heat moving through her body at speed, sending her hormones into overdrive—all because his hand was on her arm.

Run that by me again.

'Let's move on. I am here—between shifts, at any rate. Someone has to make sure you don't mow the lawns or finish chopping that firewood for a few days.'

'I get it. You'll be sleeping most of the day. I can't do any noisy activities.'

Take your hand away before I fold into you for an activity not on your mind, let the need churning through me take over completely and make you laugh—at me.

'Morning, big brother.' Chantelle strolled into the kitchen. 'Sleep well?'

Michael instantly dropped his hand and stepped back—too quickly if the groan that ripped across his lips was an indicator. The knuckles grabbing the edge of the counter were white.

Steph pulled a chair close. Put a hand on his shoulder. 'Sit.'

He didn't let go of the counter as he sagged onto the chair. 'Silly bu—'

'Small boy present,' Chantelle warned.

'Uncle Mike, I lost Bugsy. Mummy found him in my bed.' Aaron stood in front of Michael, tiny hands on narrow hips as he stared at his uncle. 'Do you want Bugsy to make you better?'

'Sure.'

Steph kept her hand on Michael's shoulder until the tension had seeped out of him. 'Want me to change your dressing?'

'After breakfast,' Michael said. 'Don't need everyone getting in on the show.'

Zac's paws clicked on the tiles as he came to nudge up against Steph's thigh. Her other hand automatically dropped to his head.

A laugh had her snapping her head up. 'What?'

Chantelle was grinning like a cat with the cream as her gaze roamed from her brother to Steph to Zac and back to Michael. 'Nothing. Come and have a shower, Aaron. I need to get you to the daycare centre and me to class.'

Thank goodness Aaron raced away towards the bathroom and Chantelle had to follow before he got into mischief or Steph might have brained her for that smartass look in her eyes, as if she thought there was something going down between her and Michael.

'What do you want for breakfast?' she asked the man causing her endless problems with her hormones and her heart—and his sister.

'I'll fix something when you've gone to bed.'

'Since I'm going to eat before doing that, I can make double. Scrambled eggs suit?' As if she'd leave him sitting there with nothing to eat. 'I can make enough for everybody.'

So much for cereal and easy.

'Don't start running around after my sister,'

he snapped. 'She's more than capable of look-ing after herself.'

'Hey, cut it out. It's no big deal to cook enough for four. Besides, I'd look a prize cow if I didn't at least offer.'

What was his problem with his sister? Only one way to find out, and as she could hear the shower and Aaron's chatter through the wall she had no compunction about not remaining quiet.

'You're not pleased Chantelle's here?'

Michael tipped his head back and stared up at the ceiling.

For a long moment she thought that was all the answer she was getting, so she went to the fridge to get eggs and cream. She'd make enough for everybody, and if it wasn't eaten she'd have an egg sandwich for nightshift.

'It's not like her to help me.'

'But you're close?' They seemed to be, despite the moments of tension she'd observed. 'Or is it that you like looking out for Chantelle but don't want to be on the receiving end of the same?'

He fixed her with a troubled gaze. 'I've always got her back—and Aaron's.'

She'd run with that—avoid the other idea since it didn't seem to be sitting well with him. 'The father's not in the picture?'

'He took off before Aaron was born. Which was a very good thing. At the time Chantelle was in a bad place, but pregnancy made her stop and take note of the appalling life she was leading, forced her to rethink her future.'

'Hence university? That takes courage and strength. You've got to be proud of her.'

'I am.' Michael blinked as though he hadn't considered that before. 'But some days I wish she'd sort out the rest of her act instead of expecting me to always be there, picking up the pieces.'

Collecting Aaron from daycare when she was late being one of those pieces. Steph got it, but if it was her she'd be happy to grab what time she could with her nephew.

'She made you dinner, stayed the night. That suggests a two-way helpline going on here.'

Michael blinked again, muttered slowly, 'Yes, she did…'

Through the wall she heard the shower stop running so returned her attention to making breakfast. But while whisking cream into eggs and adding salt and pepper she was still seeing Michael's face—filled with pain when he moved too quickly, with love when he looked at his nephew, exasperation when he talked about his sister. And confusion when he touched her arm.

The guy had a lot going on in that head. How much of a distraction was she? Did he ever think about their affair and wonder if he'd made the right decision to call it off? Did he want to spend time with her, get to know her better? Or was he glad he'd made the call and now couldn't wait to be back on his feet and have her gone?

Of course he was.

The whisk flicked raw egg over the bench and the front of her uniform jersey and she cursed. She needed to get it cleaned for work that night. Banging the bowl in the microwave, she quickly wiped the bench before tugging her jersey over her head. And found Michael's gaze locked on her—make that on her breasts as they stretched the buttons of her shirt.

At least that was what she thought he was staring at. Judging by the lust in his eyes, she knew she was right. *He wanted her.*

She still didn't know for how long. Didn't know if he needed one night in bed with her or a month's worth.

Then he shook his head and glanced at the microwave, which was beeping. And now she had another answer. He might be feeling the need, but he wasn't following through. Not because of his injury, but because he just *wasn't.* Didn't do the commitment thing.

She hated the fact that she could still hear those chill, heartbreaking words as if he'd said them yesterday.

'I am not interested in a long-term relationship, with you or anybody.'

Blunt. Honest. Hurtful.

Carefully stirring the eggs, she swallowed the second lump in her throat of the morning.

Have breakfast, take Zac for a walk, then hit the pillow and get a few hours' shut-eye. Let the day unfold as intended.

Her new and boringly normal life was reality. Shoving the bowl back in the microwave she pressed the start button. That was how it was.

You forgot about changing Michael's dressing, seeing and touching his thigh, feeling his heat while you're at it.

No, she hadn't—she was deliberately avoiding thinking about it, that was all.

Nor had she forgotten that she was going to change his mind about trying to make him fall for her. Once she'd worked out how to go about it.

Aha. She already had Chantelle's attention. Help might be around the corner.

Michael swallowed some painkillers and hobbled on his crutch to the lounge and the TV remote. Breakfast had been a shambles. Not the food, but Steph had gone into a funk for no reason he could fathom, and that had annoyed the hell out of him.

He liked having her around. No denying it. When she walked in the door after a night on the ambulance it seemed as though she'd always been doing that—as if she belonged here, with him.

Which was a perfectly good reason why he

should be pleased her mood had changed and he was being kept at a distance.

When she'd changed his dressing she'd been aloof, the ultimate professional. Definitely not a friend or an ex-lover. Then she'd yawned—so unprofessional he'd have laughed if he hadn't been afraid for his thigh. Exhaustion had been pulling at her shoulders, and her eyes hadn't been their usual sparkling toffee shade. Night shifts did that to people not used to them, and Stephanie was still getting into her stride.

Zac had had his walk, he'd been offered more tea on their return, and then Stephanie had disappeared down the hallway to the bathroom for a shower. She hadn't come to see him before she'd shut herself in the bedroom she was using. Was she sound asleep? Or tossing and turning in search of oblivion?

He could remember the sheer frustration of not being able to sleep after a long night shift in the department when he was training. It had felt as though his body had been craving sleep so much it couldn't shut down.

The TV came to life and he waved the remote in the general direction of the channel button. What was happening in the world? Flicking channels, he listened to the news without really hearing it. Today he couldn't drag up any sympathy or interest or outrage for the heinous crimes people were committing against each other all

around the world. This morning his weary mind
kept wandering to Stephanie. Cursing the fact
that she should be annoying even when she
wasn't near.

He'd have enjoyed another bath—needed one
really, if that pungent sweaty odour was anything
to go by—but it would have to wait until Stephanie woke up, hopefully in an improved mood. If
only he could bath himself, but taking a tumble
on those tiles would not be a good look, and it
wouldn't help with getting back to work ASAP.
And it would certainly not be sensible—which
he was prone to be about most things.

Though not about Stephanie Roberts.

Oh, yeah? Meaning...?

Meaning that somehow she'd managed to get
under his skin again. Could be she'd never actually got out from there. She definitely had him
thinking about her far too often, in ways that had
nothing to do with work or being friends. His
mind, overruled by his body, kept fixating on
the stunning curves her uniform did nothing to
hide. He knew those curves, the silky skin cov-
ering them, Steph's heated reaction to his fingers
and lips skimming over her body.

Big mistake, having her stay here. But he'd
really, truly believed he didn't want a long-term
relationship. Had he been lying to himself?
Whether he had or not, it didn't change the fact
the he was still frightened of failure. Falling in

love and then crashing and burning had been painful once—it would be catastrophic a second time.

Five to nine. How was he going to fill in the hours till Stephanie got up? How long would she sleep? She'd told Zac she'd take him for another walk later in the day. She hadn't told *him* anything more than that she'd change the dressings again when she got up. Oh, yeah, there'd been mention of a shopping trip before dinner.

Dinner. Now, there was a challenge. What if he put a meal together? It wasn't as though he didn't know his way around the kitchen. He just never bothered for himself. But Steph should eat a proper meal before leaving for work. He only had one working hand at the moment, but surely it couldn't be too difficult to create something.

Shoving himself up off the couch, he felt pain shooting through his leg, and that had him questioning the ridiculous idea and reminding him why he was here and not at work in the ED. *Tough.* He'd give it his best. He had all day.

Zac lumbered to his feet and followed, getting in the way in the kitchen, bumping into Michael's injured leg. Gasping, Michael tripped, put weight on that leg, felt pain in the wound. The air turned blue.

Zac sat on his haunches, his tongue lolling and his eyes fixed on Michael, oblivious to the problem he'd caused.

Sinking onto a kitchen chair, Michael wiped the sweat off his brow and breathed deep, absorbing the pain, and worked to ease the tightness in his thigh muscles.

Talk about being a geriatric. This was ridiculous. In his rugby days whenever he'd got knocked down he shrug the pain aside and get up to continue running around the paddock. He was not as fit as he'd been then, for sure. Using the gym and going for runs was not the same as the hours and hours he and his teammates had put in to keep their bodies in tip-top condition.

'You all right?' Stephanie swished into the kitchen, an empty glass in hand, thick bathrobe wrapped around her body, hiding all those superb curves he adored.

'Sure.'

As she filled the glass from the fridge water dispenser she studied him. 'You're very pale.'

'Hard to get a tan in winter.'

'Smart Aleck.' There was a hint of a smile on those luscious lips.

'You been asleep at all?'

'Not yet. I find it hard, being out of routine. It's years since I did nights, and I was never good at sleeping during the day.' She sat down beside him, with no sign of the funk that had been gripping her before. 'Let me look at that leg.'

'It's fine.'

'As any red-blooded, full-of-testosterone male would say.'

'Sometimes I think you forget that I'm a doctor and quite capable of dealing with my own injuries.'

But he was already tugging his track pants down to his knees. Oh, so sexy… Track pants were *not* a turn-on. Definitely more comfortable at the moment, though. That thigh did not need fitted trousers holding it tight, and nor did another part of his anatomy that had a tendency to get hyped up whenever Steph was close.

Which was why he'd slipped a pair of boxers on when he'd got up. Having Stephanie noticing his apparatus while she changed dressings wouldn't be good. Especially as said apparatus had a tendency to tighten, thicken, and show its feelings for her without any input from his brain. He leaned forward, arms folded low over his abdomen in case that particular reaction got carried away now.

'Since we're looking at it, I'll change the dressing and save the discomfort later.'

She was so gentle removing the gauze pad he didn't feel a thing. But then he was concentrating on not noticing how her thick hair fell over her cheek, and on not breathing in that honey scent. He cursed silently. Reaction happening.

'Do you think you could make me a cup of tea?' *Now. Immediately.*

'Give me a minute and I'll put the kettle on.'

A minute? That was a lifetime in this condition.

'Great.' *Not.*

In a minute he was going to be tied up with need. Need that overrode everything else his body was feeling as those gentle fingers cleaned a smear of blood from the stitches holding him together. That was what he needed to stay strong and sane—stitches in his head. Talk about going stark raving mad...

What could he talk about that was totally unrelated to skin and fingers and tightening muscles? 'Do you eat pasta?'

Ouch. Her finger had slipped, rubbed the top of some of the stitches. Served him right.

'Love it.'

Love what? Oh, pasta. Of course. 'Then that's what I'll make.'

'Pardon? Michael, are you all right?' She laid her palm on his forehead. 'No temperature,' she quipped. 'But it seems you've forgotten I'm here because you can't get around easily. You sure can't make pasta. Unless... I get it. Where's the menu? I'll pick what I want and you phone the order in later with yours.'

That palm was soft, warm, soothing...not to mention downright sexy. Who knew his forehead could feel hot and intense and needy from Stephanie's touch? Not him. But then around

Steph he was learning about quite a few things
he'd never have believed possible. Like how he
wanted to make her a meal to show how much
he appreciated having her here while he was in-
capacitated, how happy it made him to know she
cared enough to be in his house when she clearly
didn't want to be.

'Michael? Menu?'

'There isn't one.'

He loved how her eyes widened, that brown
shade looking soft and gooey, like caramel melt-
ing in a pan. Or was that his stomach feeling
gooey? Like a besotted kid dealing with puppy
love?

'Now I know I can't go back to bed. You'll get
up to something that's not good for your wrist
or your leg if I do.'

A smile broke out, lifting her cheeks, lightening those eyes further. Warming his insides,
sending his heart into some strange unknown
rhythm, giving him hope. *Hope?* For what? A
future different from the one he'd known since
that promise to his dad? One where everything
worked out? A future with Stephanie in it permanently?

She did this to him. Rattled him, knocked his
beliefs sideways so he rethought everything he
lived by. She wasn't good for him, pushing his
boundaries wide.

Stephanie was so close the corners of their

chairs touched. He only had to lean forward a little, use his good hand to gently pull her nearer and then put a finger under her chin to lift her head and those full smiling lips were right there, under his mouth, startled into silence, into inaction.

His mouth was on hers, kissing her as though this was his last kiss ever, giving everything he had, taking whatever she had to offer. As her lips softened under his he relaxed and gave up trying to remain in control of his manhood...of anything. No point. He was going with it for all it was worth—enjoying the moment, forgetting the consequences.

Pain tore through his leg.

Michael jerked back, gulped, bit down on the oath rolling across his tongue. *What the—?* This was the worst pain yet.

'Zac, move away.' Steph stood up fast, her chair rocking back as she reached for the dog's collar and tugged him aside. 'Keep away from Michael's leg.'

Her eyes glistened as she hovered next to Michael.

'I'm so sorry. I shouldn't have brought him with me.'

'What else were you supposed to do?'

The dog was her pet—she couldn't give him back for a few days even if there was someone to return him to.

Deep breath, keep everything normal. 'Don't worry. These things happen. He doesn't understand.'

'Yes, but—'

He reached for her free hand, threaded his fingers between hers. Hadn't they just experienced the most amazing, heart-stopping kiss? Forget the blasted dog.

'Yes, but nothing. I'm fine.'

Physically he was in agony. Mentally he wasn't any better.

When Patricia had left him he'd known he'd never risk marriage again. Divorce was in the genes. So was taking responsibility seriously. While Carly had now gone offshore and seemed happy and content, wasn't getting into major difficulties, he knew that could change any day. But it was Chantelle who gave him the most concern. She pushed herself too hard and the cracks were starting to appear. He had to be there for her, and more importantly for Aaron, if everything turned to custard again.

It wasn't the first time she'd got so far with sorting out her life and then gone off the rails. He had to admit that this time she did seem to have more control over her emotions. And if that was so he might be able to have some life for himself. But he still couldn't risk hurting Stephanie and breaking his own heart as well.

He was thinking all this while holding Stephanie's hand. He looked at her, saw uncertainty, but couldn't let go. He wanted her. Forget all the reasons he'd just put up for not doing this. He wanted her.

'Stephanie?' Her name slipped off his tongue as easily as melted chocolate.

Her eyes widened and her fingers tightened briefly around his. Then she stepped away. 'Not a good idea, Michael.'

Her tongue slid across her lips, refuting her words. She wanted him. Fire glinted in her eyes.

'I agree. Doesn't mean we have to be sensible, though.'

Her hands slapped onto her hips, her fingers white where they dug in. 'I'm the most sensible woman you've ever met.'

'I can change that.'

Her lips twitched, but the intensity in her eyes didn't lighten. 'I know you can, Michael, but it's not happening.'

She turned and walked away, down to the bedroom.

Before he heard the door click shut he'd swear she said, *'Not today.'*

CHAPTER EIGHT

SLEEP WOULD BE impossible now. Steph shoved her legs into her jeans, jerked them up, tugged her jersey over her head and dragged a brush through her hair. Her skin was hot, her mouth soft where Michael's lips had touched hers. Her body throbbed persistently.

Why had she pulled away?

Certainly not because she hadn't wanted his kiss. Quite the opposite. She hadn't been able to get enough.

Her finger touched her mouth, circled slowly. The man only had to kiss her to turn her into a blithering wreck. But wasn't that what she wanted? *Yes.* Definitely. And more.

So why was she taking Zac for a walk instead? When she'd decided to make a play for Michael? To try and win him over?

He'd been kissing her as if he meant to go through with the promise of hot, knee-melting, mind-blanking sex. But she didn't want sex with Michael. She wanted to make love. Yes, he had been right there, on the same line, but he was aiming to have sex, not make love.

Short-term for Michael. For ever for her.

'Zac,' she called as she made her way to the front door, avoiding the kitchen where she presumed Michael still sat. Or not.

What did it matter? He didn't need her fussing over his leg at the moment. Sometimes she'd swear he didn't want her helping at all. But that could be because of what hung in the air between them, what had burst out into the open minutes ago. Did she affect him as he did her? He couldn't have been thinking straight or he'd never have kissed her in the first place. Having sex or making love would be impossible with that leg.

A gentle head-butt to her thigh brought her back to reality. A walk with the dog, not hanging out with Michael, was the order of the morning. Then maybe she'd actually go to bed—alone— and get some shut-eye. Otherwise the night ahead would be long and taxing.

They headed out to the road. In her hurry to get away Steph had forgotten to grab her car keys, but no way was she going back inside to that kitchen for them. Because of her cowardice Zac would not be getting to run free this morning. A few laps of the block was his lot. Not that he looked unhappy. Did this dog even do unhappy? He whimpered in his sleep, yet never pined at the door for his previous owner, or tried to head towards his old home when they were out walking.

Maybe there was a lesson for her in there somewhere.

Steph upped her pace, stretching out her legs, puffing short breaths into the chilly air. She should've worn a jacket. Not going back for that either.

Michael and his kisses were something else. Until now she'd thought she'd do anything to get more, to have the whole follow-up thing between the sheets, or in the shower, over the table.

Seemed she didn't know herself very well.

Seemed she wasn't prepared to sell her soul to get her man.

No, apparently she was going to have to find another way to his heart.

Remember Stephanie mightn't stay in Auckland very long, despite her protestations to the contrary.

Michael stood up slowly, easing the kinks out of his body, but not the heat and tension from his groin. That was taking a while to die down, mocking him from below.

He swore, reminding himself that he hadn't been the one to pull away. Stephanie had. When her blood had been pounding through her veins and desire had gleamed in her eyes, softened her mouth, tightened that already firm body. He cursed her for being the wise one. Because, whichever way he looked at it, he shouldn't have been kissing her—let alone thinking of heading to his bedroom with her.

Blaming her made him feel like a heel when he wanted to feel better about himself. Gratitude should be filling his tense body—not unresolved need for Stephanie.

More need than sex.

Michael jerked, and swore again as his thigh complained in the only way it knew how. No, he did not want a relationship that he couldn't walk away from at any time. Not with Stephanie. What about sex with friendship thrown in? *Yeah. Right.* Like that was going to happen. He couldn't do that to either of them.

Opening the pantry, he glared around at the shelves, banged the doors shut in frustration. The cupboards were bare except for toddler food. Likewise the fridge and freezer. When had he got so slack he didn't do a proper grocery shop?

Digging in a drawer, he found a pad and pen. Time to get his act together—turn this place into a home, not a dosshouse for toddlers, paramedics and out-of-order doctors.

'What are you doing?'

Michael gritted his teeth as he knotted his shoelace tight. He hadn't heard Stephanie return. Zac had let him down—no head-butting to warn him.

'Getting ready to go shopping.'

And he'd taken a bath—carefully, not wanting to end up sprawled across the floor and unable to get up on his own.

'I beg your pardon?' Annoyance tightened her mouth. 'You're meant to be resting that leg, remember?'

'There's the rest of the day for that. Right now I need some groceries.' He nodded at the pad on the table. 'Quite a few. I've ordered a taxi to take me to the supermarket and hang around until I'm done.'

Which could take for ever if his leg didn't play ball.

'Cancel it. I'll get these.'

'You need sleep. I'll manage. Anyway I like to do my own shopping.'

I do? Since when?

Since one stubborn woman had started shaking her head at him and picking up *his* list.

'Which company did you call?'

She dug her phone out of the backside-outlining pocket of her jeans.

'If I can't do it for you then I'm going with you. It will be a lot more comfortable in your car, and since this list is longer than your arm you might want to take a break—at which point I can finish the job while you wait outside.'

'I hate it when you're right.' He picked up his phone and called the taxi company.

You give in too easily, mate.

Yeah, well, he was learning there was no other way with Stephanie. Especially when she made a load of sense—which she did too often for comfort.

'What about your sleep? I don't want you zoning out over a patient tonight because of me.'

'I'll be fine. I can catch some zeds this afternoon. If it's all right with you I'll stop in at my house on the way back for a couple of things I need.'

'No problem.'

He liked it that she didn't gloat when she'd won. He liked a lot of things about her. Including the backside he was following out to his car. Most of all he liked having her back in town, in his life. Though could he trust that to be anything more than temporary?

When she'd left the department and Auckland he'd been bereft. Not to mention guilt-laden, believing he'd been instrumental in her decision to go. It had hurt despite it being his own fault. And that had been after only two weeks together.

Would he do it again if their feelings escalated into another fling? Cut her off before they got too involved? Yes—without a doubt. That was how he protected himself. Last time Stephanie had done a runner. Never to be heard of again by him until now.

Except that wasn't true…

His mind flashed to the card tucked in the back of a drawer in his desk down in the spare room he called an office when Aaron wasn't sleeping in there. A card with a scrawled message of congratulations for qualifying as an emergency specialist last year, signed *Steph* followed by three 'X's. Not hot, *take me* kisses like those that sometimes followed him into sleep, but kisses that evoked memories he didn't like to acknowledge.

As he buckled his seatbelt his phone rang. Chantelle. Was she working tonight? Needing him to look after Aaron as per usual? He could give it a crack…

Kidding yourself, mate. Being irresponsible. What if you fall and can't get up? How's that looking out for Aaron?

Frustration made him groan. 'Hey, Chantelle. How's your day going?'

'Great. Remember that exam I sat last week? I got top marks.'

'Go, you! That's fantastic.' Pride filled his chest and he turned to Stephanie. 'Chantelle got top marks in her law paper last week.'

Stephanie leaned close and said loudly, 'Congratulations, Chantelle. Brilliant result.'

His sister laughed. 'I'm stoked! Michael, I

just called to say I'm cooking dinner tonight.
Crumbed chicken legs with roast vegetables.
We'll also be staying over since Steph's working. Do you need me to get anything from the
supermarket?'

'Got it under control. We're heading there
now.' Chantelle was helping him out for a second
night in a row? She wanted something, for sure.

'You sure that's a good idea?' Chantelle asked.
'There will be trundlers going wild and toddlers
running around not giving a care for an old guy
on crutches. I can get whatever you need.'

'I do not need babysitting twenty-four hours a
day,' he said grumpily, not telling his sister that
Stephanie had already made sure he didn't go
alone. Bloody women—outmanoeuvring him
all too easily.

Chantelle laughed.

Beside him Stephanie chuckled as she drove.

'Give me a break, you two.'

They both laughed harder. Ignoring them was
the only way to go. But he couldn't deny the
warmth filtering in at the thought that they both
cared.

Then Chantelle quietened. 'Michael, stop
pushing me away. Let me do something for you
for a change.'

She paused. Gathering strength for battle?

'I'll see you round six-thirty. Bye.'

Gone.

Michael stared at the instrument in his hand. What had just happened? Chantelle wanted to stand up and be counted as a helpful sister? No, there had to be more to this, but damned if he knew what. There was only one way to find out—play the wait-and-see game. It wasn't as if he had to be anywhere today apart from the supermarket. At least with his sister the wait wouldn't take for ever, patience not being part of her make-up.

Patience was supposed to be a virtue. But it was one Michael found he didn't have any more of than his sister.

Not when pensioners were clearly blind and in charge of shopping carts. Not when office workers in a hurry to get their lunch thought their getting served at the deli counter took precedence over everyone else. Not when Stephanie insisted on taking his shopping list and running up and down the aisles collecting items without consulting him on which coffee he preferred, how many grains he liked in his bread, and whether he preferred sirloin to fillet steak.

'Give me that,' he growled as she put a pack of steak in the trolley he was apparently supposed to be leaning against when he got tired of swinging around the place on his crutches.

Reaching to get the pack, he ignored the stab of pain from bumping his thigh against the unforgiving corner of the shopping cart. Fillet steak was for girls. A decent, thick sirloin was the only steak he'd have in his house. After returning Stephanie's choice to the cabinet he searched through every pack of sirloin to find the perfect piece of meat.

'This one,' he said with satisfaction, his mouth watering at the thought of eating steak for dinner. Except it would have to wait. His sister was on dinner duty tonight, and he couldn't find it in himself to override her offer. It wouldn't be fair when she was already busy and going out of her way for him.

Chicken it was tonight. Tomorrow he'd be in charge of his kitchen and the steak.

By the time Stephanie had loaded all the bags of groceries into the boot of his car and then loaded him into the passenger seat he was shattered.

'Thanks for doing this. I'd have given up long before I got to the end of my list.'

'I know.'

Okay, so she could gloat.

'We won't go to my place. I can do that on the way to work.'

It was in the opposite direction to the ambulance base.

'What? And deprive me of an outing?' He grinned. 'It's been years since I spent a whole day and night at home, let alone two. I'm going stir crazy.'

'If you're sure?'

Somewhere amongst the cereals and the tinned vegetables she'd lightened up on him. He was back in favour—if only as someone she had to look after in a friendly manner. That kiss had been filed away somewhere in that beautiful head. Hopefully she'd think about it some more—when he was out of the firing line.

'Of course I'm sure.'

Leave it…say no more.

'Stephanie, about earlier…?' He was doing a lot of this apologising stuff lately.

'Drop it, Michael. We're adults. We make mistakes. Now we move on.'

And the car, mirroring her words, bunny-hopped down the gap between rows of parked cars to the corner leading out onto the main road, where finally Stephanie got herself, or at least his car, under control.

Neither said a word for the ten minutes it took to reach her house. Her hands gripped the steering wheel as if it was about to get away and she hunched forward, her eyes darting left, right, ahead, left and right again, as she'd have been taught on the ambulances.

He hadn't been there before, and her house came as a surprise. An early twentieth-century villa surrounded by established trees and over-long grass, it was delightful and reminded him of his grandparents' home. The gardens were minimal—probably because she'd rented the place out while she'd been away.

'It's lovely.'

And nothing like the home he'd have thought Stephanie would live in. These villas came with the continuous maintenance required by wooden window frames, lack of good insulation, and open fires that looked wonderful as they belched smoke and little heat.

Steph sat back in her seat and stared out and around. 'Yes, I fell for it the moment Freddy and I walked up the drive.'

Her voice was low, but not as sad as he'd have expected. She was doing fine.

'It was going to be perfect for us and those babies we wanted. The big bedrooms, massive lounge, all this lawn for swings and a sandpit, a vegetable garden out the back.'

Her gaze slowly tracked from one side of the section to the other, seeing things he could only guess at.

Michael's heart slowed. This house had been her dream, had held all her wishes and ambitions. An unfulfilled dream.

Reaching for her hand, he said, 'I'm sorry.' He really was.

Startled eyes turned to him. 'It's okay. I've mostly moved on, but there are times when something flips me back to then. Like the other day, with those prem babies. I think it's all part of settling back into Auckland—back into my old life without actually living that life again.'

'Do you want to?' He held his breath.

A soft smile broke out. 'No.' Another glance at her property. 'And I mean that. Like I told you, Freddy and I are history. It was a good marriage that didn't survive the stress of my infertility. I don't want to go back to what I had. I want to grab the future, make the most of what I *do* have, and not waste energy rueing my losses.'

He couldn't breathe. Couldn't talk. Couldn't even move. She was so brave, and he knew that courage had come from what had gone on in her life. Her future was here, unfolding day by day.

She hadn't been ready for him two years ago. He'd hurt her by calling an end to their affair, but she wouldn't have been able to cope with a full-on, permanent relationship then. She'd had to get away from the cloak that was Auckland and her family and a job she'd lost herself in.

'I won't be a minute.' She opened her door.

'Mind if I come in? I'd like to see around your home.' He wanted to see her style. Modern or classic? Were there lots of books on shelves? Little ornaments in cabinets?

'You just like knocking that leg, getting in and out of the car.' Her smile widened and she was at his door in a flash, a hand offering him balance as he climbed out. 'Don't even think of offering to mow the lawns. I know they're too long, but I'll get them done at the weekend.'

'Wouldn't think of it,' he fibbed.

She was safe at the moment anyway.

Steph chuckled. 'You can do better than that. I know you're itching to get my mower out of the shed.' Although it was a machine that needed new sparkplugs and its blades sharpened.

'At the moment I'd be happy to sweep your drive.'

'You're bored. I get it. You're also impatient.'

Why was he laughing at that?

'Come on—I'll give you the grand tour.'

She looked around the yard. There was a heap of work to be done before spring, when the trees would start sprouting. The hedge was out of control and the gardens were a riot of weeds. Exhaustion sank through her. She just couldn't dredge up the enthusiasm those tasks had brought her in the past.

Inside, the temperature could have done with being cranked up, but with her being away and the fire not lit it wasn't going to happen. Besides, she'd run out of firewood days ago and hadn't got around to ordering in another load, what with everything else she'd been doing. She knew that if she told her dad there'd be wood stacked in her shed by the end of the day. *If* she told him. She wouldn't.

Michael was right behind her as she entered the sitting room.

'You could hold a party for a hundred people in here and have room to spare.' He was looking around at the high ceilings, panelled walls, her minimal furniture tucked into one small space in front of the fireplace.

'Sixty-five, actually.' She shivered, and not only because it was freezing in here. 'My twenty-sixth birthday.'

It had been a wonderful night, and she'd been so happy. Now this room only gave her goose-bumps.

'Come and look at the rest.'

Ten minutes later she was locking her front door, with a bag of clothes over her shoulder and the truth opening her eyes. This house no longer excited her. It was too big, too empty, too old. It was the past. Now she wanted to sell it and start again, with small and cosy, modern and easy-care. But could she afford it in Auckland's current volatile housing market, where prices rose by the day?

Only one way to find out.

She'd talk to a real estate agent later.

CHAPTER NINE

'WHIPPITY-DO, FINALLY HOME...' Steph sang off-key as she let herself into Michael's house next morning. It had been a quiet shift compared to the previous one. She'd even managed to snatch an hour and a half sleep upstairs in one of the staff bedrooms towards the end.

A yawn warned her that that wasn't enough, but it would get her through the next hour or so while she made breakfast for everyone, and walked Zac, and checked out Michael's leg.

Michael.

Yesterday's incendiary kiss had been a warning. She could not continue to do this and come out unscathed. But then she'd known that when she'd decided to go for him. The only difference between before that kiss and after was that now she knew she'd be looking out for herself along the way.

Zac bounded out from the kitchen, his thick tail flipping from side to side, endangering a large ceramic pot in the entranceway.

'Hey, good to see you too,' she said as she rubbed his solid head. Being welcomed home was cool—and nice. 'Thanks for choosing my door to slobber all over the other day.'

Michael was already up and in the kitchen, filling the kettle. 'Morning. How was your night?'

'No major emergencies for once. How about you? Get some sleep?'

He wouldn't admit it if the pain had kept him awake but she had to ask.

'Plenty. I've been out running a lap of the block, given my car an oil change, and got a cake cooking in the oven.' His mouth was tight, his lips white, but there was mischief in his eyes.

Dropping her bag and keys on the table she grinned. 'Good. What're you planning on for dinner tonight?'

Two mugs with teabags in them sat on the bench.

'Chantelle gone already?'

'She forgot to get Aaron clean clothes last night before coming here so she had to head away early.'

Opening the fridge to get eggs, Steph spotted cooked chicken drumsticks and took one. 'You *did* make dinner.'

Though there hadn't been any chicken in that shopping yesterday.

Biting into the cold meat she felt her mouth water. 'Yum.'

'No, I didn't. Apparently I have a sister who's quite capable of cooking.'

'Why wouldn't she be? Look at Aaron—he's not malnourished.'

'Takeout food could do that.' Scepticism resonated in his voice.

'Come on, Michael, that's not fair.'

Glancing across at him she felt her mouth dry. Even in loose trackies and a sweatshirt he looked delectable. Way tastier than the chicken.

'You don't know what you're talking about,' he muttered. 'Chantelle has never been able to look after herself properly—has always had my number on speed dial…number one at that.'

'This is the sister who's been happy to stay here with you for the last two nights?'

'The very one.'

'You're not making a lot of sense. The moment Chantelle heard about your accident she was here for you.'

Opening the fridge, she stole another drumstick. To hell with eggs on toast. This was way quicker and easier. No cleaning up after involved.

'That did surprise me, I admit.' He got up to make the tea. 'It's not like her. I've always been there to help her, not the other way round. Same went for Carly, my other sister, until she went to England. "Michael, sort this." "Michael, can you do that?" Of course I'm happy to help—always have been.'

'Not so happy being on the receiving end, though.'

Did he think he had a role to play in his sisters' lives that only went one way? Back when she'd worked in the ED with him everyone had heard about his sisters and how he was always running around after them.

'Maybe Chantelle's saying thanks for everything you've done for her. Or maybe she's just acting how family is supposed to—being there when you need help.'

He stirred and stirred the teabags in the boiling water. 'You know nothing about my family.'

Putting a hand over his to stop the incessant stirring, she said, 'Then tell me.'

I want to know about them, about you, about how you all click.

He shrugged her hand off, spooned out the teabags and added milk to the mix. 'My dad left my mum when I was seven. I got to stay with him at weekends. He remarried and along came Carly and Chantelle. I adored them right from the first time I laid eyes on them. I finally had siblings and life was less lonely when I was hanging out at my dad's house.'

He sank onto his chair, sipped the tea.

'Then Dad moved on again. I was thirteen, and he told me I had to step up and take care of my sisters because he couldn't always be there for them. I wasn't always there for them either since they lived with their mother, and me with mine a few streets away. At least he made it convenient in that respect.'

That stank. Talk about handing over responsibility… Some parent *that* man had turned out to be.

Steph took her mug to the table and sat down beside Michael. 'I can see you taking on that responsibility.' It was Michael to a tee. Or had being handed that role forged who he'd become? Forced him to take on the persona he didn't know how to let go of?

'There was a time when Chantelle lived on the edge. She was irresponsible and a little bit crazy.'

'And you haven't accepted that might be over now?' *Hang on.* 'You don't blame yourself?'

'I didn't see the bad crowd she'd got in with for what it was until it was too late.'

Yes, he was still definitely taking the fall for Chantelle. 'Does she blame you?'

'Of course not. But that doesn't exonerate me. I gave my word I'd be there for my sisters no matter what.'

Steph took a gulp of tea. Okay, she was probably about to get kicked out—banished to the other side of the city. But…

'You were thirteen and the girls' half-brother. Not their father or their mother.' Where was that woman in all this? 'You didn't have to shoulder all the responsibility. And even if you thought you had to when they were young they're adults now. They can look out for themselves.'

Michael stood up, snatched at his crutches as they started to slide towards the floor. 'You're wrong. It's what I do, and what I will continue to do for Aaron as well. It's why I live like this. There is no room for anyone else. There is no time for any more with my family and my job keeping me busy.'

Message received, loud and clear. No time for *her*. Minutes for kissing, even more for sex, but nothing else. Certainly not involvement. And this was the man she loved, wanted to be with for the rest of her life.

'You don't want a family of your own?'

Hurt filled his dark gaze even as he shook his head in denial. 'You didn't hear what I said?'

'Yes, Michael, I did. But I don't believe it all. I get it that you think you have to be there for your family. I don't understand why you can't have both. Others do and manage very well. It's how families work.' Hers did anyway.

'Not mine.' He started for the door.

Steph stopped him with a hand on his arm. 'You sure that you're not hiding behind this responsibility? That there's not something else keeping you from finding happiness, having the life you want?'

Something slipped into his gaze which she

couldn't read, but it suggested she'd touched a raw wound.

'Stick to your day job, Stephanie. You're so much better at that than trying to change me into what you think I should be.'

Low blow. Probably deserved, but unfair. She loved him, and he had just closed the gate on going anywhere with that. Closed it and pad-locked it. Why had she said anything? But she was always honest, no matter the consequences, and that was what she'd been just now. The price was huge, but at least she could live with herself.

If it was possible to live with a broken heart.

Where was Zac's lead? She had to get away for half an hour or she'd say something she'd regret for ever. If she already hadn't.

Michael cracked eggs into a bowl too hard and had to pick out pieces of shell. That was what listening to Stephanie did—wound him up something terrible.

He picked up the whisk and began beating the eggs. His injured wrist wasn't very helpful in holding the bowl. Ignoring it, he whisked harder, faster. Gooey egg flicked over his sweatshirt.

Whisk.

The bowl slid sideways. Over the edge of the bench onto the tiles.

He stared down at the yellow goo, the shards of crockery which had been a bowl moments before, and wanted to roar. To shout at the world. To blame someone, *something*, for the wound in his thigh hurting like stink, for the ache in his sprained wrist, for the mess splattered over his track pants and on his floor.

For the words pinging back and forth in his head.

'You sure that you're not hiding behind this responsibility? That there's not something else keeping you from finding happiness, having the life you want?'

He cursed out loud. No, he *wasn't* sure. He knew that if he had his sister and his nephew to keep him busy and involved he could cope with being single and living in this big house alone, because they added noise whenever they dropped by. But that was coping, not enjoying, and definitely not loving someone special.

Patricia had taken him to the cleaners when she'd walked out on him. He hadn't minded so much when she'd demanded half his money. But he'd hated it that she slept with one of his teammates and that she'd gone to the press, who had been only too eager to hear the 'inside story' she'd chose to make up about their marriage.

He'd been broken-hearted that the future he'd hoped would bring him love and a family had dissolved into nothing but recriminations. That he really did have the family divorce gene.

That gooey puddle on the floor wasn't getting any smaller.

Stephanie wanted all the things he couldn't give her. Commitment beyond everything. Which meant his wanting a repeat fling with her was unrealistic. He would not deliberately hurt her, and that was the fastest way he knew how to.

So he needed to get on with cleaning up the mess and forget how her body had felt up against his yesterday. Had it been only yesterday that he'd kissed her? Seemed timeless...as though that kiss had brought all the previous ones forward to wreak havoc in his head, make him hungry for future kisses.

After filling the sink with cold water he tried to bend down and scoop up egg with the dishcloth. His leg protested. Spots flickered across his eyes.

Straightening, he pulled a chair close and eased himself down on that. Now he could reach the mess, but he had to stand to rinse the cloth. Just as well he didn't have to be anywhere in a hurry. Up, down...up down.

Those spots behind his eyes were annoying, but the sooner he was done here the sooner they'd disappear.

At the park Steph unclipped Zac's lead to let him run free. He barked and leapt in the air, his tail going in all directions, before chasing after a blackbird that was happily digging for worms under a tree nearby.

Her heart lifted momentarily. Why had the dog sought her out? It wasn't as though she lived next door to his owner. Not even close to her house.

Which reminded her...

She punched her speed dial. 'Hi, Dad. How's things?'

'Your mum has got me sorting through the shed in the hope I'll get rid of what she calls rubbish and I think of as treasure. What about you? Settled in with your friend?'

Far from it.

'It's all good. We hardly see each other—though that's about to change now I'm on days off. Can you give me Bill's number? Or get him to ring me? I want to talk real estate with him.'

'I'm seeing him at golf this afternoon. I'll give him your number. What are you thinking?'

Her parents would support her in a move if it eventuated. They'd often said her house was too much for her to look after on her own.

'That I might look for something low-maintenance. Wouldn't mind a kitchen and a bathroom that were designed in the last couple of years, not nearly a century ago.'

'Your oven's better than a coal range!'

Her dad's laughter always warmed her, but today it was a struggle. Michael had got to her in ways she hadn't expected, and it hurt that they'd never get together properly…permanently.

'Only because I put a new one in before I went away.'

She followed Zac around the park as she talked to her dad. If only she could talk about Michael—but what was the point? There was nothing anyone could do to fix her heart. No one but Michael, and she knew where she stood with him.

Right now her feet were itching to run. Out of town, out of the country, as far from Michael as it was possible to get. As far from the source of pain in her stomach, her head, her heart. So much for the best-laid plans. She really had blown those to shreds.

But she had no intention of taking off for other places. She'd come home for good, and that was where she was staying. A new house, maybe, but not a new location. Another tick on her list? Absolutely. She was getting a few of those now. Only the big one she wanted was evasive.

Bark, bark.

Zac bounded up, skidded to a stop at her feet, causing her to trip around him. 'Easy, beautiful…' Then, 'Dad, I'd better get going. Have a great game. Love you.'

Clipping Zac's lead onto his collar, she glanced at her watch. Ten o'clock. The day stretched out interminably. Sleep was required, but that meant heading back to Michael's. At the moment being in the same space as him would crush her, though she *was* meant to be there for him.

She had to find someone else to take her place—fast. If only she had Chantelle's phone number she could apply pressure to get his sister to take a couple of days off from university. Waiting until the end of the day seemed impossible—too long and too filled with worry that she wouldn't be able to convince the woman.

Why hadn't they swapped numbers? It was usually the first thing she did when she met someone she knew she'd see again. But then nothing had been normal these past couple of days.

What about Max or Jock? Surely one of them could take Michael home for day or two? They'd insisted she have their numbers, and had phoned a couple of times to ask after Michael, only to follow up by giving him hell about being lame.

She'd try them. And a district nurse could call in to change his dressings.

'No can do, Steph,' Jock said as soon as she'd put his mind at rest about Michael's condition. 'My in-laws are coming to stay today.'

Max wasn't any more helpful. 'Love to help, but my parents are coming to stay.'

In-laws and parents all coming to stay on the same day? *Jerks.* They were forcing her to stay with *their* mate. As for why—she wasn't going there. Michael needed new friends.

Back on the road, Steph headed for coffee and a muffin, then hit the supermarket, visited the vet clinic to make an appointment for Zac to be checked over, then spent time in a dress shop trying on and discarding an array of outfits she had no need of.

It wasn't until Zac began whimpering and looking distressed that she knew she could no longer put off going back to Michael's house.

The moment she opened the front door a feeling of apprehension slithered down her spine.

'Michael?'

It was too quiet.

'Michael?'

He wasn't answering. He wouldn't have gone out without leaving her note. He wouldn't have gone out *at all*. Would he?

He lay on the floor, half against the cupboards beneath the kitchen sink, looking very sorry for himself. And very angry.

'Michael—what happened?' She nudged aside a chair that had tipped over near him. She dropped to her knees beside him, lifted his arm to feel for his pulse.

He pulled his arm free. 'I'm fine. Just need a hand up.'

'*I'll* tell you whether you're all right.' She grabbed his wrist again.

'I slipped. That's all. Nothing to get in a flap about.'

'Says the man who would berate *any* of his patients who didn't follow his instructions on how to look after themselves.'

Now it was her turn to get angry.

'What were you *doing*?'

There was something sticky on the floor. And bits of the bowl she'd been going to scramble eggs in before she'd flounced out of here.

'You were scrambling eggs?'

'I was hungry. Can't a bloke do anything for himself?'

'Not when his wrist's sprained and his thigh has layers of stitches that a knock could damage—let alone what falling to the floor might do.' She let go his wrist. 'Your pulse is normal.'

'That's good.' Relief flicked through his gaze.

'What? Is there something you're not telling me?'

'Help me up, will you?'

'Are you going to faint all over me?'

'No.' Michael sighed. 'I promise. I dropped the bowl of eggs and I was trying to wipe up the resultant mess but it wasn't working. I couldn't reach properly. And then I stepped in the egg and my feet went out from under me. That's all.'

'That's more than enough. Are you sure you didn't faint?'

There was still that relief shining in his eyes.

'Positive. Though there were a few spots before my eyes earlier, when I was bent over trying to touch the floor. But they didn't cause me to up-end.'

He sounded definite, and since his pulse couldn't lie she let the matter drop.

But she'd have to keep an eye on him all day. There went her sleep...

She lifted his good arm to put over her shoulder and wound her arm around his waist. 'Come on. Let's get you back on your feet.'

Michael held on to the edge of the bench with one hand and between them he was soon upright—though his face was white and his grip on her shoulder tight.

'Thanks, Steph. I wouldn't have blamed you for leaving me there.'

'It was tempting.' She smiled, wanting to get back on side with him. 'Shall I give some more eggs a whirl?'

'You going to join me?' Caution laced his words, held him still.

'Those drumsticks hardly touched the sides!'

It didn't take long to clean up the mess and start again.

'I rang Max and Jock to see if one of them could give you a bed for a couple of nights. You don't need me to change those bandages. Any nurse could do it. But seems they've both got family coming to stay.'

Michael rolled his eyes. 'Their parents all live within ten kilometres of their houses.'

'I figured. Anyway, I reckon you'd probably go spare in someone else's house so I'm going to stay for a couple more nights.'

Had she really just said that? She needed her head read.

He pushed up on to his feet, walked across so he stood directly in front of her. His hands caught hers. 'About that earlier conversation... We were stepping on things I don't like to talk about, even though I started it. Can we put it behind us while you're here? You know a little more about me, but it doesn't have to change anything.'

Too late. Everything had changed.

'I've forgotten what you said already. Just try not fall on the floor again, will you? I might be taller than average, but weightlifting was never my favourite sport.'

If they could muddle along together without any more upsets until he was safe on his own then she'd stay. She mightn't be able to persuade him to look at her as a potential future wife, but she'd take what she could get.

Pathetic. But true.

CHAPTER TEN

'SIT, ZAC.' STEPH STOOD at the side of the road by Michael's house, waiting for Zac to park his haunches. 'Good boy.'

She shivered in the cool, wet night air and hunched into her jacket. Winter was the pits. If she hadn't been so restless she might've stayed inside and made Zac miss out on a walk. Another walk. This was his third today. Every time she needed to put space between her and Michael she picked up the lead.

She wondered what Bill had come up with as a sale price on her house. He was going round there after golf. Hopefully he'd leave a message on her phone. Her phone that was on Michael's bench—not her brightest move.

When she got back, three cars crowded the driveway. Max and Jock were clearly visiting, and Chantelle was here for dinner. Steph now had her number, and had texted her to ask her to come round.

In light of their conversation about hiding behind his duties to his family, she wanted Michael to take a look at Chantelle when neither of them were on edge about doing things for each other. Of course it would probably all backfire and she'd be the one going home tonight.

The guys dropping in was a bonus. They'd lighten the atmosphere with their jokes and cheek. She'd like to meet their wives sometime…

Hello? That would mean being more involved with Michael.

'Hey, Steph, get this into you.'

Max must have seen her coming up the drive, because he stood in the doorway with a large glass of wine in his hand.

'Michael said you like a Pinot Gris, same as him.'

'Sure do—thanks. Is he still grumpy?' she asked as she shrugged out of her windbreaker. 'He brought in a bucket of logs earlier, hopping on one foot and swinging his crutch precariously. It's a given that he dropped the bucket on his foot.'

Max scowled. 'Stubborn idiot. But no worries. I've brought in enough wood to last you a couple of days, and Jock chopped up some more for later on.'

A couple of days?

'He's already pushing the boundaries on how

much he can do, which is a fair indicator that I won't be needed much longer.'

Zac plonked down on the mat in front of the fire, stretching out his paws and laying his head on top of them, his eyes fixed on Michael as if this was home, thank you very much.

Sorry, boy, but this is temporary.

'I see the dog's made himself comfortable.' Jock grinned. 'Getting to be like a regular family around here.'

'Butt out,' Michael growled, with no smile within range.

For once his friends didn't say another word. Instead they busied themselves with pouring drinks, pulling chairs closer to the fireplace and tipping chips into a bowl.

'Your phone's rung twice,' Michael told her when she sat down by the fire. 'I tried to answer it…'

'But you were too slow?' She laughed.

'I hope it wasn't anything important.'

Michael was watching her closely. Looking for what?

Her laughter died. It was hard to keep it rolling when the person she was trying to share it with was looking like a storm on the horizon.

'I doubt it.'

Probably Bill. She went to get her phone, saw

that there was a phone message and a text from the agent.

Looking up, her eyes clashed with Michael's. Still under scrutiny. She shoved the phone in her pocket. She'd call back when everyone had left. Right now it was fun to have company and dilute the Michael atmosphere.

Sipping her wine, she sighed. 'Just what the doctor ordered.'

'Not *this* doctor,' Michael quipped, appearing to relax now that she'd put her phone away.

Aaron climbed up onto Michael's good knee, attracting his attention, and she relaxed further. It was fun to be able sit and talk and not be on edge about everything she said.

After Max and Jock had left, making comments about her and Michael to wind up their friend, Chantelle cooked rice to go with the slow-cooked pork Steph had made and poured them both another glass of wine to enjoy over dinner.

At nine Chantelle gathered Aaron from his bed and headed for the front door. 'Thanks for dinner, Steph. Are you okay staying for another night or two?'

'I think so.'

'Give me a shout if you change your mind!'

And Michael's sister was gone.

Steph closed and locked the door, suddenly all her energy gone. Time for a decent night's sleep.

Which was really pathetic, considering she was sharing a house with the man she loved.

'Stephanie? Are you all right?' Michael appeared before her.

'Couldn't be better.' She pushed away from the door. 'Let's do your dressing.'

Then she could escape to her room down the hall and bury her head under the pillow until the alarm told her it was time to get up and go to work.

'As far as nightcaps go, that has to be the worst I've ever been offered,' Michael grunted, before heading to the bathroom and those bandages.

But it had to be done, and the sooner the better, because then he could find something to watch on TV and stop wondering why Auckland's number one real estate salesman was trying to get in touch with Stephanie.

He'd seen the man's name flash up on her phone's screen. It had been hard not to demand what was going on. If Stephanie was thinking about leaving town again he'd be devastated.

'Your injury's looking a lot better,' Steph commented minutes later. 'The swelling's going down. You'll be running soon.'

'With or without the crutch?' He intended leaving it aside as much as possible from now on.

'There—done and dusted.' She looked up at him. 'What's bothering you?'

He could lie, say nothing, but he didn't. 'That phone call from Bill Summers.'

Her face lightened. 'I need to call him back now that everyone's gone.'

'A bit late, isn't it?'

'He's an insomniac. Dad refuses to share a room with him on golf trips because the lights never go off.' Her phone was already in her hand as she stood up. 'He went round to do an evaluation on my house this afternoon. I wonder what he's going to tell me.'

Michael stood too. 'Are you selling?'

'Thinking about it… Bill? It's Stephanie. How did you get on?'

Michael watched the emotions flitting across her face. Mostly surprise and excitement, and his heart sank. *Yep, definitely selling.*

Unable to listen to any more, he stepped out of the bathroom and headed for the sitting room. He cursed her. Stephanie was making this harder by the minute. He mightn't be ready to take a risk with his heart, but he suspected it was too late—that it was fully engaged with her. He sure as hell didn't want her leaving town again. But what right did he have to ask her not to?

I'm a flight risk.

Yeah, he'd heard that, and then she'd added,

'But not again'. Seemed she didn't know what she was doing.

'Wow, that's pretty darned good.'

The woman who was winding him up dropped into the seat opposite.

'Bill has given me the price he thinks he can get for my house and it's higher than I'd ever have expected.'

'That's good.' *No, it wasn't.*

'Sure is. Especially when he says I can get a house that meets my criteria for similar money in the same suburb.'

What? 'What do you mean, get a house that meets your criteria?'

Her smile grew. 'I haven't felt right in that house since I got back. It's not mine now. I've had tenants there and it feels different. I've started moving on. I want warm and modern.' Her gaze cruised around his state-of-the-art lounge. 'Some place I can call home. I don't feel like that about my place now.'

'It's a house, not a home.' His heart was lifting slowly, warily, and the weight holding it down was going.

'Exactly.' She was staring at him. 'You thought I was running away again, didn't you?'

'Yes.'

She closed her eyes and her breasts rose. Her hands gripped her thighs. Then she eyeballed him. 'I will never do that again. It didn't solve anything last time, and isn't likely to if I do it again.'

'What needs solving?'

She looked away, staring at the far wall. Looked back to him, hope and sadness filling that brown gaze. 'My future.' She stood up. 'I'm going to bed to catch up on sleep.'

Future. Bed.

The two words stuck in his mind. One he could do nothing about. The other…? It wasn't what she'd meant. He knew that. But could he really continue to fight the attraction between them? Would embracing it help lift that sadness? For a while at least?

He pushed up onto his feet. 'Steph?'

Steph couldn't have moved if the house had been on fire. There was something in Michael's eyes that dared her to step closer, to touch him, to hold him, to— She didn't know what…only knew that she had to find out.

Her hand was on his. His skin was warm and smooth. Her skin was on fire. Standing this close put temptation right in front of her. Temptation she was not going to deny herself.

Michael entwined his fingers with hers as he stood up. 'Steph…' he breathed, long and slow.

Was 'Steph' good? Or bad? When he called

her Stephanie she felt special. Right now she had no idea how to feel about that. He was so close… so, so close. She only had to lean forward an inch and her forehead would be lying on his chest.

A finger touched her chin, tipped her head up so her gaze clashed with his. 'You're beautiful,' he whispered as his mouth lowered to hers. 'May I?'

Raising onto her toes was her only answer. Words were a waste of effort and breath when all she wanted was to kiss him, to be kissed senseless by him.

He tasted good. Of man and dinner and the lemon dessert his sister had brought. What more could a woman want? She pushed higher, closer, needing more of him. All of him. She ignored the consequences. Tonight she'd take what she could and the rest she could think about tomorrow.

Her arms slipped around his neck, holding him so that he couldn't get away if he suddenly changed his mind. Then Michael had his arms around her, pulling her up against his body, his chest against her peaking nipples, his abs nudging her belly, touching her from chin to toes. His mouth joined in and she was lost. Not that she intended changing her mind. Not this time.

His hands were under her jersey and splayed across her back, each finger a soft pad against her feverish skin. She remembered this. How she heated in an instant whenever he touched her skin. The explosion that would come when his fingers touched her sex. This was what she'd been hankering after, fighting off. A Michael moment. A *long* Michael moment when he would kiss her blind, caress her and tease her wild, and finally take her to a place that was special beyond description.

He'd shown her a part of herself she hadn't known existed. No wonder she wanted him so badly... No wonder she loved him.

Steph stilled, her breath caught in the back of her throat. This was wrong. *Yes*, she loved Michael. *No*, it wasn't going anywhere. So she should be heading for the door right about now. But she wanted him. Her body craved him. Her trembling legs were a clue. Her blood charged around her veins, thumping, hot, in need of what only Michael could give her.

'Stephanie...' Michael's voice was a whisper. 'Look at me.'

She bit back a curse. He'd stopped kissing her. Opening her eyes, she stared into his, saw his need for her, his love and care, and the worry that she might back off.

'You okay with this?' he asked softly.

Her head dipped. 'Yes. Very.'

More than okay. No matter the outcome, she was going to follow through and make love with this man she loved with all her heart. She wanted and needed to. But most of all she had to show him how she felt, and this was the ultimate way.

Pulling Michael's head close again, she returned to kissing him, and being kissed back, until the heat between them was incendiary... until her body was plastered against his and her hands were under the waistband of his jeans and sliding slowly down, down, down.

'Bedroom,' he croaked, pulling those lips away and wrapping his arm around her waist before heading down the hall to that enormous bed he slept in.

'Bedroom,' she agreed. 'Bed.'

Soft, warm, and about to be trashed as they poured their feelings out.

'This isn't going to be easy,' Michael said.

'What? *Oh.*' She'd completely forgotten about the wound to his thigh. Which didn't make her a good person, did it? 'Want to stop?'

'No.' Raising her jersey, he pulled it over her head. 'And I'm not going to unless you ask me to.'

'No chance.'

Her fingers were arguing with the zipper of his jeans. She'd go and find a pair of scissors in a minute...

'Let me.'

Zip down and her hands were pushing the

jeans down over his hips, over his butt, his thighs, his… That injury *was* a problem.

'What if I bump your leg? Cause pain?'

'Then you can kiss it better.'

With one arm under her knees and the other at her shoulders he swung her up and lowered her to the bed, quickly following to lie beside her, pulling her across his body, keeping his injured leg clear.

Spreading her hand over his belly, she felt a shiver of anticipation rock her. She was making love with Michael. This was for real. No longer a memory or a dream. It was *real*. His length was hard, strong, silky to the touch. Up, down…up down. Urgency drove her. She needed this. But what if he suddenly changed his mind? Remembered why he'd walked away last time?

'Not so fast,' he gasped, and reached between her legs for her moist spot.

'I like fast,' she whispered, colouring as she heard herself. Talking about sex wasn't her strong point.

'Yeah, right…' he growled, and then kissed her to show how he intended to continue, his tongue plunging into her mouth, retreating, plunging again.

Steph gave herself over to the pressure building inside her, along her veins, in her core, in the air surrounding them, in her hands.

This was making love with Michael. This was *perfect*. For now. And it was a start. And she wasn't finished.

Her hand slid over his waist, down his belly…

When her phone woke her at five Steph was not ready to get up and face a day on the ambulance. No, lying here curled up to Michael was the better option. The best option. The only one.

Except she couldn't ignore work.

The weight of his arm over her waist, his soft breath on her neck, his length tightening against her backside even before his eyes opened…all excited her.

Twisting around in his arms, she kissed his chin, then his mouth. 'Good morning, sunshine.'

She hadn't felt this good in for ever.

'Morning,' he grunted, pecking her cheek before giving her a quick squeeze and rolling onto his back. His gaze was fixed somewhere above them.

Oh-oh. Morning-after regrets? Great. Thanks a lot.

Though she only had herself to blame. It was to be expected after his revelation about not getting into a permanent relationship. Had she been silly enough to think he might change his mind after they'd made love? She really didn't know men at all.

Not true. She'd known it was a risk—that he was unlikely to change his mind over some hot sex. And for him it *would* have been sex. For her, making love had never seemed so wonderful. But he knew she wanted a second chance at marriage, and he wouldn't be putting his hand up.

With a heavy heart she sat up and tugged the bedcovers over her breasts. Sharing was all fine and good when they both were enjoying themselves, but she wasn't about to parade around for him to see all her working parts if he was going to say, *Bye-bye, nice having spent the night together, but now it's time for you to leave.*

She couldn't help the curse that fell from her lips. 'What's your problem?' she demanded, hoping he might say something,—anything—so that she could talk with him.

'I don't want to hurt you, Stephanie.'

Back to her full name. She'd used to like him using it, but now, after last night and the way he'd dragged out the word 'Steph' in a moment of ecstasy, she'd changed her mind.

'I got the picture when you told me about your responsibilities. You do not want a relationship that involves more than sex. I don't understand it, but I knew about it when I willingly came in here with you last night.'

'This can't go anywhere.'

Even though this was nothing new she felt her heart die. It was doing that a lot these days.

'Then why did you make love to me?'

'I couldn't help myself. Nothing would've stopped me unless you'd demanded I back off. I've wanted you from the moment I saw you on your first day back. You do that to me.'

Michael reached up and wrapped her in his arms. His forehead touched hers and she waited for his lips to settle on hers.

'I've been selfish and I've hurt you. I regret that more than you can ever understand.'

His arms dropped away, leaving her chilled. And lonely. So much for thinking she could do this.

Sliding her feet sideways, she found the floor and the clothes they'd tossed aside in the heat of the moment last night. Grabbing Michael's shirt, she hauled it over her head. It was bigger to hide in than her fitted jersey that only reached her hips.

His shirt smelled of the same scents that had teased her and taunted her, heightened her anticipation every time they'd made love throughout the night. It made her want to cry. But big girls didn't do that—not when they'd been warned they were taking a risk.

Would he notice if she kept it? Hid it in her

bag and took it away with her? If he did he'd probably have her locked up on a lunacy charge.

'Right, I'd better get a wiggle on or I'll be late.'

He didn't disagree. 'I should be able to fix my own dressing this morning.'

Dismissed.

The chill intensified, clawed down her spine, while another, icier one surrounded her heart, dulled any warmth she had for him. Safety measures finally taking shape? If only they weren't too late.

'I've got time to do it before I go.' There was more acid in her words than intended, but, hey, she was hurting here. 'And to make breakfast,' she snapped.

'Stephanie, stop.' Michael was struggling to untangle his legs from the sheet. 'I'm sorry. I was trying to make it easier for you. That's all.'

'Fine.'

He still didn't want her leaping back into bed with him, though. Couldn't he have pretended everything was fine at least until she'd left for work?

Not likely. Brutally honest, was Michael.

The shower took for ever to heat up, giving her time to stare in the mirror at her pale face and sad eyes. When was she going to learn? Michael had made it as clear as the Fiordland Sounds water that he had no intention of settling down, and even clearer that it would never be with her.

So she must grow a backbone, think of last night as the adventure she'd known it would be before she'd kissed him with all the intensity of her love for him. Be happy about the exquisite sensations he had created within her, the new memories. Or if not happy, then for goodness' sake she must at least stop looking so glum. It didn't become her.

A face like the one staring back at her from the mirror would scare the pants off any patient who had the misfortune of having her turn up to load them into the ambulance. They'd run even if they had broken their leg.

'Multiple vehicle accident on the harbour bridge,' Kath informed her as she dumped her bag in the staffroom forty-five minutes later. 'We're on. Along with two other crews who already left.'

No time for feeling sorry for herself, then. *Perfect.*

Steph dug deep for her friendly face, mentally preparing for what they might find on the bridge and crossing her fingers that no one was fatally injured, or even close.

'The traffic's going to be diabolical at this hour. Wonder how many lanes are closed?'

Three of the four southbound lanes were

cordoned off and traffic in the remaining one was barely moving. Traffic cops directed them through the cordon to park behind the other ambulances.

'Take the grey car,' Joe, an advanced paramedic and the site leader, instructed them. 'The driver's oxygen saturation levels are dropping. The fire crew is working to lift the steering wheel off her. She's your priority, followed by the passenger beside her. She has facial trauma but is lucid and aware of what's going on, and doesn't appear to have internal injuries.'

Steph approached their patients, the gear pack bumping on her hips. Nothing like an emergency to focus her.

'Hello. I'm Steph, a paramedic,' she told the driver, who stared at her through glazed eyes. 'I'm going to attach a mask to your face so we can give you some oxygen. Okay?'

She didn't wait for a nod, just got on with the job. There was a lot to do before the firemen got this woman out of her metal prison.

Kath read the BP. 'Low. Ninety on sixty. The sats are still dropping. We might have to intubate once she's lifted out of here.'

They worked quickly, minimising the trauma, intubating, crossing their fingers they wouldn't lose the woman. Steph doubted she'd be able to cope with that on top of her bad start to the day.

'Ready for us to lift the steering wheel?' a fireman asked.

'Yes.' Kath nodded.

Steph stayed beside the woman, keeping a watch on the heart monitor in case the easing pressure caused a blood haemorrhage from internal damage they hadn't been able to assess. A wedding ring on the woman's third finger glinted in the sun. They had to keep her alive—otherwise there was a man out there who'd lose the love of his life. *Not happening.* There might be children who needed their mother to come home too.

'We need the stretcher,' Kath called to someone, and immediately it was there, waiting while they continued working on their patient.

Then they were lifting the woman and wheeling her towards the helicopter waiting at the start of the bridge.

'Good luck.' Steph called quietly, before turning to the passenger and starting over.

No sooner had Kath called base to log off that call than they were speeding down Dominion Road to a bus versus pedestrian accident. Followed by a call-out to a man who'd been washed off the rocks in Freeman's Bay as he attempted to land a fish and had broken his leg instead.

Lunchtime was a joke—snatched mouthfuls of bread rolls filled with ham and salad as they raced to another road accident, and then a child who'd fallen off the jungle gym at school, and then a mother who'd knocked a pot of boiling water off the stove and over her toddler.

CHAPTER ELEVEN

MICHAEL PUT THE phone down after his fourth call of the morning. He'd bathed, changed his dressing, dressed in jeans and a shirt. His leather jacket was slung over a chair. He'd drunk a plungerful of strong coffee and for the first time in days felt half human.

Only half. The scene this morning in bed with Stephanie still had to be resolved. But he was working on that.

That look of despair and hurt she'd tried to hide had pierced him deep.

Last night she'd told him she was doing something about where she lived, meaning she was moving forward, wasn't letting the past hold her back. Throughout the night as he'd made love with her, held as she slept, as he'd breathed in honey, felt need deep in his stomach, he'd known excitement. And relief. Excitement and relief that she was staying—wasn't rushing away, looking for everything she already had here in her home city.

And he wanted the same. *With her.* If she was prepared to start over then he had to step up to the mark and be as courageous. Take a risk with his heart. Yes, well… That wouldn't be easy. But after three days with her in his house he knew he had to try. Three days and he was ready to admit he wanted for ever. If she'd give him a third chance. It was a lot to ask—especially when he hadn't done anything to show how much he meant it. He needed to take risks, stop hiding behind Chantelle and Aaron.

Yes, Steph, you're right. I do use them to protect myself from letting anyone else close enough to hurt me. My sisters can cause me grief, but they'll never leave me for ever.

'Sorry, Zac, my boy, but you're going to be tied up for the next few hours. There are things I have to do.' *For Steph, me, and the future.*

Thump, thump of his tail on the tiles.

'No, I'm not taking you for a walk. I'm going out. Alone.'

Not quite alone. He was having lunch with Chantelle and Aaron at a family-friendly restaurant where the wee guy could play amongst the bouncy balls. He was going to have a long overdue talk with his sister. It wouldn't be easy, but it had to be done.

Toot-toot.

The taxi was in his drive. 'That's my cue, Zac.'

The dog followed him outside to the garden shed to be tied up.

'See you soon. Cross your paws for me to get this sorted out right.'

At the restaurant Aaron charged him, but he was ready, his crutches put aside so he could swing the little guy up in his arms. 'Hey, man! You going to eat chicken and chips for lunch?'

'Yes, Uncle Mike. Lots and lots.'

Warmth filled Michael. He loved this kid to bits. And he loved the owner of those arms going round him now.

'Chantelle...' *Sniff.*

'Choking up's new for you.' She gave him a kiss on the cheek. 'Steph's really got to you.'

'Pardon?'

'Come on. You're the only one in the dark over this. You and maybe Steph.' She took Aaron from him. 'Let's put you in with those bouncy balls while Uncle Mike and I have a chat.'

'Coffee?' Might as well overdose and give his body the kick that it apparently needed. It seemed everyone except him knew what his heart was thinking. Did *Steph* know? She hadn't backed off last night when he'd reached for her.

His heart lifted.

Or was she just following through on the physical with no thought for the future?

His heart dropped back to his gut.

'Coffee's the best I'm going to get to drink in here,' his sister grinned. 'You'd better order food while you're at it. A certain boy isn't going to last long before he wants to eat.'

With coffee in front of them, and the food order being processed, Michael found that he didn't know where to start.

'I'll give you a clue,' Chantelle said. 'Patricia did you more damage than you've ever admitted to yourself.'

'She did that,' he agreed. 'But I probably made it easy for her.'

'Because of Dad and his divorces, your mum and ours and their break-ups. Mine came later, but it only proved you were right to think divorce was a given for Laings.'

'You knew I thought that?'

He'd never talked about any of this with his sisters. Never talked about anything from back when they were growing up and dealing with their parents' take on commitment.

'You're an open book to Carly and me.'

It wasn't hard to laugh. Another surprise. 'Thanks a lot.'

'So… Steph?'

'She accused me of hiding behind my responsibilities.'

'You've always done that.'

He had to agree with both women. 'It was how I coped.'

The divorce gene thing wasn't really his problem—not a major one. It was the pain of the betrayal that had led to his divorce. The killing off of his dreams for family and love.

Steph would never do that. It was there in her demeanour, in the way she stood up to him when she thought he was wrong, the way she had moved in to help him when she already had enough on her plate.

The food order arrived.

'Eat up. I've got things to do.'

He could only hope he wasn't too late.

Driving away from the base at the end of shift, Steph struggled to find any energy. After a night full of activity and little sleep, her day at work had topped up her exhaustion levels. But it was the nagging feeling that she couldn't face another night at Michael's house without breaking down that really got to her.

As for stopping at the supermarket to get something to prepare for dinner, and then actually cooking it—forget it. Soup in a can sounded the perfect solution. And if Michael didn't like soup, too bad. She'd heat and eat it, and go to sleep.

Zac. Damn. She had to take him for a walk.

He'd be excited and leaping all over her when she stepped inside.

Her legs ached at the thought of doing anything other than curling up on the couch but her heart sighed. *Bring it on. Zac's your new life.*

And she did love the dog—got all teary just thinking about how he seemed to have selected her for *his* future. As though he had an unerring sense of her need for a stability that matched his. So of course they'd go for a walk. It was their together time—all part of the deal she'd made with herself for her new life.

Anyway, it would get her away from sitting in the kitchen, facing Michael, eating soup in silence. At the moment she was beyond talking to him as if nothing hurt, nothing worried her. As if she was a woman who'd had a wonderful night and moved on.

The front door opened and Zac bounded out before she'd locked her car. 'Hey, boy, how's things?' His ears were like silk against her palms.

'He's been for a walk,' Michael called from the porch.

'Not alone, I hope?' she answered through her surprise that Michael was waiting for her *and* talking to her.

A sharp bark of laughter. 'No. I took him.'

Her surprise deepened and she studied Michael as she hauled herself up the steps. 'How

did that go for you? You're still upright and looking in reasonable working order.'

She guessed she couldn't avoid talking to him,
and Zac didn't exactly stay to heel for his walks,
preferring to leap about and wind the lead around
her legs.

'We managed. I am getting back up to speed.'
He held the door wide, then closed it behind her.
'Dinner's ordered for seven-thirty.'

Her grocery bag bumped her knee. 'Anything
would beat tomato soup.'

What was going on? He'd taken Zac for a walk
and sorted dinner.

'You must be feeling a lot better.'

Maybe sex had been the recharge he'd needed
to start getting back on his feet. Pity it hadn't
worked like that for her.

She headed for the kitchen.

'Steph, wait. About this morning. We need
to talk.'

She shook her head at him. 'Why? You were
being honest. I don't like that you want nothing
to do with me after what I thought was a wonderful night, but at least you weren't playing games.'

Since when did she do such transparent honesty? Lay her feelings out there for him to know?

Honesty deserved honesty.

Yeah, but her heart deserved protection too.

Shoving his hand through his hair made the

thick curls stand up. 'I didn't want to push you away, which is why I did it.'

Steph grimaced. 'You're fighting me. Us.'

'Yes. I was.'

He was watching her as if he couldn't get enough of her—but that had to be wishful thinking on her part. He hadn't wanted a bar of her that morning.

'I'm going to take a shower. You want to put this in the pantry?' She tried to hand him the supermarket bag.

He ignored it. 'The days you've been staying here I've found I listen out for you coming home after work, after every walk you take with Zac. It's strange, considering I've lived alone for twelve years. Not counting the time Chantelle and Aaron spend with me. That's different.'

She wasn't getting this. He'd made absolutely certain she knew there was no place for her in his life beyond the bedroom last night.

'I'll be blunt. I don't understand.'

He took her hand, led her into the sitting room and gently pushed her in a chair. 'Would you like a glass of wine?'

He wasn't waiting for an answer, had glasses already standing on the sideboard. The snapping sound of the cap on a bottle of their favourite Pinot Gris was loud in the sudden silence.

'Are you dodging my question that wasn't a question?'

'Here.'

A full glass appeared in the line of her troubled vision.

'I'm not sure I need that. I'm shattered and I intend eating and going to bed. Alone.'

That last word had sneaked out unintended. But now she'd put it there she felt some of her tension slip away. She was in control. Whatever Michael wanted she wasn't interested—because it wouldn't involve marriage and for ever.

Then she lifted her gaze and really looked at him. At the man who'd made love to her last night. It hadn't been just sex—not from her position. Badly worded, but she knew her own meaning. This was the man who had held her tenderly when she was upset, who had watched her back even when she'd asked him not to, who had joined her in leaning against the wall in the ED when her heart was cracking without even knowing what it was all about.

A deep sadness and despair washed into her. Why did she have to fall for a man who didn't do marriage? Of course she was interested—but not dumb enough to believe that would solve everything. Only staying ahead of him would do that.

A loud pounding on the front door gave her the opportunity to escape while she collected

her thoughts. A small man was on the bottom
step, hoping from one foot to the other. 'Lady,
you ambulance person?'

'Yes, I am. What's wrong?'

She knew the moment Michael come up beside her, felt his warmth.

'My wife. She very sick. Come quick.'

'I'm coming too,' Michael muttered. 'Don't
go inside until I'm there. I'll get the first aid kit.'

The one that rated right up there with those
they used on the ambulance.

'Good idea,' Steph agreed as she followed the
stranger down the path. 'Where are we going?'

'Over road. White house. We underneath.'

'Underneath' turned out to be a pokey flat,
damp and cold, with mildew the main colour on
the walls. Steph shivered.

'Here my wife.'

A small woman lay on a narrow bed, huddled
under a dirty blanket. Her breathing sounds were
erratic. The face peering up at her was covered
in a red rash.

'How long has your wife been like this?'

'Hour.'

Bleeding heck. Why had he taken so long to
knock on Michael's door?

'Hello, I'm Steph—a paramedic. Can you hear
me?' Lifting the blanket, she gasped at the small

but very pregnant belly. 'How far along are you?
How long have you been pregnant?'

The man held up six fingers.

'Six months?'

He nodded.

Steph found a wrist, took a pulse reading.
Slightly fast. The woman was gasping for air,
taking short inhalations. Her eyes opened whenever one of them spoke, but her response to touch
was sluggish.

'Thought I said to wait outside…' Michael
handed her the BP cuff. 'Need an ambulance?'

'Yes. Rash…shortness of breath. Query ana-
phylactic shock. GCS four.'

Steph wound the cuff around the woman's arm
and pressed the button on the machine. Michael
handed her his phone. 111 was already showing
on the screen.

'I've got an allergy pen in my kit.'

Phew. 'She's six months pregnant.' That baby
had to be saved, no matter what.

'What emergency service do you require?' intoned the woman at the call centre.

'Ambulance.'

Steph was put through and rattled off the details and the address, not taking her eyes off the
woman and that baby bump. *Please be all right.
Hang in there baby, we're getting help. There's*

no way we're losing you. Her eyes watered. It seemed saving babies was her thing.

'BP's low.' Michael backed up the shock theory. 'Is your wife allergic to anything? Is there any food she can't eat? Do insect bites make her sick?' Michael asked as he tore the cover off the allergy pen.

The man standing over them looked as if his world was imploding. 'No, she good with all food. Never happen before.'

'What's that?' Steph pointed to a red swollen spot on the woman's arm. 'Looks like a bite to me.'

A quick look and Michael agreed. 'Whitetail spider?' He jammed the needle into muscle and pressed down. 'Now we watch and wait and keep the baby safe.'

A man after her own heart. 'Yes, we do,' she whispered.

Waiting sucked. But there was nothing else to do. Except…

She wrapped her hand around the woman's tiny one. 'Is this your first baby?'

The woman nodded. 'Yes,' she whispered. 'I worried about baby.'

Michael had a stethoscope pressed against the woman's bump. 'Seems all right in there,' he told the anxious parents.

Steph was as relieved as they were. Look-

ing around the dimly lit room she wondered if
a whitetail spider was the culprit. Where there
was one of those there'd be more.

'Thank you for coming,' the man said. 'We
having a girl. What's your name?' he asked
Steph. When she told him he smiled. 'We name
baby Steph.'

Tears sprang up, and she didn't bother stopping them. 'That's lovely, but you don't have to.'

In her hand the woman's fingers squeezed.
'We do. You came fast. I'm glad you live close.'

No point in explaining. Steph rubbed the back
of her free hand over her face. Where was that
ambulance? It was taking for ever to get here.

Then there was the sound of a siren, coming
nearer up the road, getting louder by the second, and Steph relaxed. Michael threw her a
warm glance and continued to keep an eye on
the woman, checking her pulse and temperature
again.

She didn't know what to make of his warmth,
but she guessed it had something to do with their
interrupted conversation.

Once they'd handed over to the paramedics,
both of whom she'd met before at the station, Michael slung his kit over his shoulder and wrapped
an arm around her waist.

'You all right?'

'Yes, I am now we've handed over. That baby will be okay, won't it?'

'Yes, Steph, that's one you don't have to worry about.'

'But what if it gets bitten once it's born when it's living there?'

'Don't go there.' Michael took her hand in his. 'I'll talk to them about getting the place sprayed for all spiders. Or maybe you should. They've fallen for you.'

If only he'd do that too.

As soon as they were inside his house he put down the kit and laid his hands on her shoulders. 'Go and have that shower you were wanting.'

'All right.'

'Your wine will keep a bit longer. So will I.'

His smile hit her in the heart.

Did this mean they'd return to the conversation they'd been stumbling around before his neighbour had banged on the door?

As they sat down in the lounge again, all scrubbed and in clean clothes, Michael had to sit on his hands, figuratively, or else he was going to leap up and scoop Stephanie into his arms and hug her until that sadness was banished for ever.

He wanted to do it. To promise her that she'd one day be a mum, to make her feel better, to obliterate her pain.

In other words he wanted to be able to wave a magic wand and make everything better in her world. But he was all out of wands, magic or not. And that wasn't what tonight was about. Suddenly he couldn't just sit here and talk about his feelings. He had to show her.

Back on his feet, he reached for her. 'Come with me.'

In the dining room he stopped, and Steph gasped as she saw the table set with silver cutlery and a floral decoration in the middle.

'What's going on?' Troubled eyes turned to him. 'Michael?'

'Dinner will be delivered any minute.'

'Pizza or Thai?' Her voice was barely there.

'Neither.'

He led her across the room and held out a chair. His hands were shaking, his heart thumping. What if he'd got this wrong? He'd die if she laughed at him.

'I rang the seafood restaurant down on the waterfront—asked for their dish of the day.'

'Since when do they do deliveries?'

'Since I begged them.'

'You're scaring me.'

I'm scaring myself.

'Don't be worried. I only want to make you happy. I told you this morning I don't want to hurt you and I meant that. Trust me?'

He held his breath and watched every expression imaginable scud across her face. When she didn't answer his heart died a little bit. He was messing this up.

'I'm wooing you.'

Fast. But hopefully not so quickly that it sent her running for the hills. He'd taken too long all ready.

She choked on the wine she'd sipped. 'You're *what*?'

'I am going to prove to you I can be the man you deserve.'

He might be making the biggest idiot of himself. Stephanie might not care enough about him—might not love him at all. But last night she'd shared her body as if it was a gift to him. He'd lost himself in her generosity, had felt he'd come home. And when he'd woken with her in his arms he'd been afraid. Afraid of winning and then losing her. Afraid of not trying hard enough.

'Why, Michael?' she squeaked. Swallowing and clearing her throat, she tried again. 'This morning I got the message loud and clear. You don't—won't—do commitment. What's changed since? Because that's important to me.'

She was trembling, and he rescued the wine glass from her fingers.

'I got honest with myself. You were right. I have been using my family as an excuse not to lay my heart on the line again. My marriage ended horribly, and while I blamed myself I also grabbed every excuse in the book not to put myself in that situation ever again.'

He swiped a finger around his collar, let some air in over his hot skin.

'Then one day I met this take-no-prisoners nurse in the ED and I've never got her out of my head since. Those two weeks we shared were so out of this world I ran. In my head, at least. But now I've stopped and turned around. I can't imagine my life without you in it in every way imaginable.'

There, he'd told her everything. Ah, no—not *everything*.

'I love you, Stephanie.'

The doorbell chimed. *Damn.* He'd waited years to open up his heart to someone and now the bloody doorbell rang. *Go figure.*

Steph reached for her wine, took a slow mouthful, savouring the delicious flavour as she gathered herself together. Had she heard right? Or was she about to wake up and find this the most horrendous dream she'd had to date?

Voices in the hallway told her she wasn't asleep. Dinner had arrived.

This was beyond scary. Michael had just told her he *loved* her.

They were the words she'd never believed she'd hear. She had her fears, but so did Michael—marriage being one of them. But he had said those three special words. Words she'd never thought she'd hear from him.

She rose on shaky legs and went to find him. He was closing the front door behind the restaurant person. She headed for him, stepped up close to place her hands on his chest. She loved this man. He needed to know that. *Now.*

Her mouth dried. Could this really be happening? He wasn't going to turn away from her again, was he?

Only one way to find out. Put her heart on the line as he'd done. *Tell him.* But he'd made a habit of pushing her away. She'd never survive if he did it again after she'd told him she loved him. As if life was going to be a beach if she *didn't…*

Okay. Deep breath.

'Michael, I love you. I have always loved you from that day you arrived in the ED. We must've clicked instantaneously without realising.'

The joy on his face as he lowered his head towards hers made her giddy. She had to hang on—tight. Then he kissed her gently, softly, lovingly. And she returned the feelings in triplicate.

Finally they dragged themselves apart and Michael took her hand, led her into the dining room and to the feast that was cooling on serving plates.

His voice quivered. 'A celebration dinner.'

'Yes, it is.' Though she wasn't hungry now. Not for food.

Tightening her hand around his, she held him still.

'You hurt me when you dumped me two years ago, but you did the right thing. I wasn't ready. I needed that time away from Auckland, away from the people who've supported me almost too much in the past. I needed to learn to stand strong on my own before I committed to someone else. Otherwise I might've dragged you down with me.'

'I worked that out recently.' Those beautiful lips widened into a heart-wrenching smile. 'But you love me, and that's all that matters. We can talk this over all night or we can kiss and make up. Kiss again, I mean.'

'I like that idea best.'

As his mouth closed over hers Steph fell into Michael, relaxed completely for the first time in for ever. She'd come home, ticked the boxes.

All except one.

Dinner was cold when they made it out of the bedroom. Wrapped in her thick bathrobe, Steph couldn't stop smiling as her body hummed after their lovemaking.

'I'll reheat this.'

'It's not going to be quite the same, but I wouldn't have it any other way.'

Michael gave her one of his toe-curling smiles as he found two clean glasses and filled them from the bottle he'd left on the sideboard.

Taking the wine he offered her, Steph made a decision. It was now or never—and she wasn't into never.

'How do you feel about us getting married?'

He blanched. 'I know I've come a long way— but not quite as far as you, it seems.'

'I'm not saying we have to rush out tomorrow to buy a marriage licence, but I want to do it one day. When I say I love you, Michael, I mean the whole deal.'

'You're right. Marriage is important.' He gulped his wine, coughed when it went down the wrong way.

She had to continue. 'It's about trust.'

'I trust you—always.'

'Sure you do. And I trust you. But what I'm saying is we have to trust *us*.' Raising her glass, she tapped her breast and then his chest. 'Us. We have to let go of the things that have hurt each of us in the past and believe in the future, trust our feelings and trust each other's.'

He nodded, his mouth lifting into a beautiful smile. 'Especially *my* feelings for the woman I know and love.'

He loved her. Air hissed over her bottom lip. That was the second time he'd told her.

'You've been showing me that for a while now, but neither of us recognised it for what it was. *Love.*'

The word slid slowly over her lips into the air between them, wrapping around them. His lips were silk on hers, tasting of wine and, yes, of love.

Was this going where she suspected it might be headed? Where she wanted, needed it to go? Excitement raised its head, heated her blood.

Down, girl. We're not there yet.

'Are you sure you can change your long-held belief so abruptly?' She didn't want him opting out tomorrow, or next month. She wouldn't survive. 'There's my infertility to consider. It would mean you won't have children of your own. Have you thought that through?'

'I have. It's quite simple. A baby would be a bonus, but not a reason to be with you. If I don't have a future with you I'll be missing out on the best chance I've ever had of the things I've dreamed about. I won't win the heart of the woman I love more than that life.'

'Oh, you've already got that.' She smiled tentatively.

He loved her. Under her ribs, her heart worked a bit harder. He was prepared to do this for her. She loved him more than she'd have believed possible. And she could give the same back. Yes, letting go of *her* belief and need wasn't that hard after all.

'We don't have to marry. I'll live with you if that's what you want.'

His head moved slowly from side to side. 'No, Stephanie. That's not happening.' He got down on bended knee and reached for her hands again. 'Stephanie Roberts, will you please do me the honour of becoming my wife?'

She'd have said yes if not for the monstrous lump blocking her throat. Throwing herself at him, wrapping her arms and legs around him tight and placing her lips on his mouth was the best answer she had at that moment.

'Is this a yes?' he murmured against her mouth.

She nodded, swallowed hard, and whispered, 'Yes, I *will* marry you.'

Tick. The final box had just been filled in.

Just as well she hadn't got around to putting the dinner in the microwave. It seemed it just wasn't a night for fine dining…

Five months later...

'Why do honeymoons have to come to an end?' Steph asked her husband as he negotiated the traffic on the northern motorway. 'I mean, if we take out the Christmas and New Year celebrations with our families and friends joining us in the beach house component, we've only had ten days of honeymoon all to ourselves.'

'You think it's all going to turn to boring and routine once we get home?' Michael smiled. 'Timetables and shifts, getting in the groceries now that you've taken up cooking, mowing the lawns so Zac doesn't get lost in the grass—stuff like that?'

'All of the above.' Something was niggling at her, and through the haze of love and fun and being with Michael it just wouldn't expose itself. 'You sure today's Sunday?'

'Afraid so. Just to remind you—we both start back at work tomorrow.'

'Yeah, yeah...'

She was looking forward to it—had missed the buzz of racing to help someone—but there'd been a much bigger buzz of another kind going on over the past weeks. Being married to Michael had turned out to be better than even her wildest dreams had allowed.

So what was wrong with her? Everything was panning out the way she'd hoped, had longed for.

Sitting beside her was the most wonderful man on the planet, who loved her exquisitely in every way possible. What more could she be wanting?

Ping.

'What's the date?'

'The fifth. Of January, in case you missed the significance of New Year's Eve.'

'The fifth?' Her mouth dried. 'It is, isn't it?' Her hands became fists on her thighs.

Couldn't be. No way. Not now. Not after all this time.

'Steph? You're worrying me.'

I'm frightening myself too.

'Sorry. It's okay.'

She'd wait till she knew for sure one way or the other—didn't want to upset Michael if she was wrong and had to retract it. She knew the pain of that all too well. He did not need to experience it just because she'd blurted out something without first verifying it.

'Now I *know* you're hiding something.'

Despite his smile there was grit in his voice that ground into her.

'You're right.' Being honest was the only way to go—pain or no pain. They'd agreed to share everything, to trust each other, to trust *them*. 'I might be pregnant.'

Michael jerked, swerving the car into the far

lane before he straightened it and got his thinking sorted. 'How late are you?'

'Only six days, but I'm never late—not even a day.'

No, this wasn't possible.

'It has to be a result of all the excitement of our wedding, and Christmas and New Year. My body has forgotten what it's meant to be doing.' Damn, this was going to hurt. 'I will not get excited. It's a false alarm.'

'Only one way to find out—and the sooner the better.'

Deliberately changing lanes for the next exit, he sped up. His mouth was grim, his eyes filled with worry when he flicked her a glance.

'Don't overthink it. Please, sweetheart.'

'It's all right. I'll be fine. I've known for a long time I can't get pregnant, so I'm not going to fall to pieces over a negative result.'

Huh? Where was the honesty in that?

At Albany, Michael pulled up outside the first pharmacy he saw and was out of the vehicle and around to Steph's door before she'd unclipped her seat belt.

Hand in hand, they raced inside. 'Where are the pregnancy test kits?' Michael called out.

All conversations stopped as staff and customers turned towards them.

'Second aisle, halfway down on the left,' a

woman in a smart navy smock answered as she made her way out from behind the counter. 'Here, let me show you. We have a few choices.'

'Just want one that shows positive!' Steph smiled, despite the fear cranking up in her tummy.

'This one is the most popular.' The woman handed her an oblong box.

Steph's hand shook as she stared at it. This was the instrument of truth. In her hand was a stick that would decide their future.

Believe in good things. Your life's turned around since you came home to Michael.

Her mouth tilted upward. 'We'll take it.'

Michael was ahead of her, his wallet in his hand, withdrawing crisp twenty-dollar notes. 'Don't worry about the change—buy as many coffees as you can.'

And then he was taking Steph's hand again and racing for the door.

'Come on, sweetheart. We're wasting time.'

The shop assistant called, 'Good luck!' which was followed by the pharmacist and the customers adding their best wishes and clapping.

The fear fell away as Steph went with the good wishes and excitement wrapping around them. The drive home took ten minutes—so much for speed limits—and felt like for ever.

But the moment they were inside the house she paused, her heart thumping. 'What if—?'

Michael's lips kissed her forehead, then her mouth. 'Let's find out.'

As the thin blue line appeared Steph shrieked and leapt in the air, before throwing herself at Michael to wrap her arms around him and kiss that grinning mouth.

'Thank you, thank you. You made me pregnant.' *Unbelievable.*

'Wow…'

His voice was filled with awe. Nothing but love shone out at her from those gorgeous eyes she fell into regularly.

'I'm going to take a photo. It can be the first thing to go into our baby album.'

She stared at the stick. Was this real? Suddenly the fear was back, turning her blood cold and lifting her skin.

'What if…?' No way could she finish the sentence.

Michael's eyes locked on hers as his warm arms wrapped around her. 'It's real, Stephanie. *Real.* We are having a baby.'

'But I couldn't get pregnant—not even with—'

A lump blocked her throat. She couldn't face waking up one morning to find the unmistakable evidence that this was all false, that she wasn't pregnant. She couldn't. Not this time.

'Shh,' he murmured against her hair. 'There's no understanding nature, darling. You and Freddy couldn't conceive together, but no cause was established. You and I, however, we're good to go.'

There was no hesitation—not a hint of doubt to mar his words.

Steph melted into him. 'Thank you for believing in this. There will be days I'll be crippled with doubt, but with you at my side I know we'll make it.'

'Trust *us*, remember?' He smiled softly before kissing her thoroughly, wiping away any trace of that fear.

EPILOGUE

THOUGH SHE NEVER admitted it out loud, the fear did taunt her and haunt her at times, forcing her to mark off every day—until day two of week thirty-eight arrived and she began cleaning the bathroom as if her life depended on it. Once every surface gleamed she headed to the kitchen, armed with rags and a spray bottle of all-purpose cleaner.

'You're exhausting me.' Michael grinned and filled the kettle. 'Sit down and I'll you make a cup of tea.'

'I don't want to sit down,' she snapped with unexpected shortness. 'The pantry needs a tidy—all that stuff in packets should be in containers—and the— Ahhh!' She sank against the bench, her hands gripping her belly.

'Steph? Oh, no. *Really?* It's happening? We're on our way?'

The pain was receding. She pulled in a deep lungful of air, wiped her hand across her forehead. 'Make that tea. This is only round one.'

No sooner had she closed her mouth than her stomach tightened painfully.

Michael's warm, reassuring hand settled on her back. 'Easy. Breathe slowly. That's it.'

'Take it *easy*? When my tummy feels like it's being split in half? I don't *think* so.'

Michael swiped the keys from the bench. 'Those two contractions were quite close. I'll phone the midwife and tell her we'll meet her at the maternity unit as soon as possible.'

'Don't pull the doctor rank,' Steph warned.

Okay, you can, but do it nicely.

'Ahhh!' Was she even going to make it to the hospital? Right now she'd swear her baby was going to make an appearance on the kitchen floor.

They made it to the maternity wing of Auckland Central with minutes to spare. Having been warned, the midwife was waiting when Michael wheeled Steph into the room, having commandeered a wheelchair from a young man who thought a sprained ankle deserved him being pushed to the ED.

The midwife examined Steph and gave her a big smile. 'This isn't going to take long. And everything's looking good.'

Steph shivered.

Don't tempt fate. Nothing's good until it's over.

'Fingers crossed.'

'Well, you're in no position to cross your legs,' Michael quipped, even while the gravity of the moment darkened his gaze. 'We're going to be fine.'

He laced his fingers through hers, wincing when the next contraction struck.

And then within minutes they really were fine.

The midwife placed the most precious gift imaginable on Steph's breast. 'Welcome to motherhood.'

She stared in awe at her baby. Tears streamed down her cheeks. 'Beautiful…'

Nine pounds. *Ouch.*

'We did it.'

Michael sat on the edge of the bed, just as absorbed with their son. 'We sure did, sweetheart.' He lightly ran the back of his finger over the tiny fist pressed into Steph's breast. 'Welcome to the world, James Samuel Laing.'

Steph snuggled into the thick pillows behind her and leaned her head on Michael's shoulder, drinking in the sight of her wee boy. A perfect bundle of joy already gripping her heart and dominating her world.

She'd just ticked the last box on her list. Okay, so she'd cheated, having added that box on the day she'd married Michael. But their love for each other had given her more hope than she'd known for a long time—enough to make her take a chance.

Enough to trust them to get it right. Together.

* * * * *

If you enjoyed this story, check out these other great reads from Sue MacKay

HER NEW YEAR BABY SURPRISE
FALLING FOR HER FAKE FIANCÉ
PREGNANT WITH THE BOSS'S BABY
RESISTING HER ARMY DOC RIVAL

All available now!